ALL THAT GLITTERS

DISCARD

IR

D1052435

NOV   2013

Westminster Public Library
3705 W. 112th Ave.
Westminster, CO 80031
www.westminsterlibrary.org

AvALon

~ Web of Magic ~

Book 2

All that Glitters

Rachel Roberts

Seven Seas

ALL THAT GLITTERS

Copyright © 2008 Red Sky Entertainment, Inc.

All rights reserved. No part of this book may be
reproduced or transmitted in any form or by any means, elec-
tronic or mechanical, including photocopying, recording, or by
any information storage and retrieval system, without written
permission from the publisher, except where permitted by law.

Published by Seven Seas Entertainment.

ISBN: 978-1-933164-67-0

Cover and interior illustrations by Allison Strom

Interior book design by
Pauline Neuwirth, Neuwirth & Associates, Inc.
Printed in USA

10 9 8 7 6 5 4 3 2

WOODS

OWL CREEK
BIRD SANCTUARY

EAGLE RIDGE

WOODS

WOODS

OWL CREEK

BAMBOO
FOREST

HIDDEN FALLS TRAIL

DEER
MEADOW

PORTAL
FIELD

MAGIC GLADE

MIRROR
LAKE

ROCKING
STONE

SWAN LAKE
TRAIL

HEDGE
MAZE

SWAN LAKE

TURTLE
BOG

CHITAKAWAY RIVER

WOLF RUN
PASS

WATER
GARDEN

ROSE
GARDENS

TOPIARY
GARDENS

ADRIANE'S
HOUSE

SCULPTURE
GARDENS

RAVENSWOOD
MANOR

MIST TRAIL

MAIN GATE

STONE WALL

MAIN ROAD

PLAYING
FIELDS

1

*K*ARA DAVIES' ROOM was a disaster of epic proportions. Discarded clothes lay everywhere. Jeans and sweaters smothered the bed. The white lace canopy above groaned under the weight of tops, blouses, and T-shirts. Capris, shorts, and leggings were piled so high up the window seat, they blocked the view of the sunset sky. Even the desk was buried under clothes. The only thing visible was the flickering screen of a pink laptop computer.

Tomorrow was the first day of seventh grade. Everything had to be perfect. Especially her outfit.

"It's gone!" Kara wailed.

"You haven't even worn it yet," a disembodied voice squeaked from beside the bed. Kara flipped a blue blazer off her bedside table, revealing a speakerphone. "Did you do a shopping bag check?"

"Tiff, I've looked everywhere!"

The laptop screen started scrolling messages from her buds in the chatroom.

credhed: emergency—kara crisis
beachbunny: just heard! Could it b more horrible 0.o
goodgollymolly: kstar, r u serious?

Kara ran her fingers across the keypad.

kstar: it's GONE! I can't find it NEwhere!!! :(

There was only one thing to do now.

"*Mom!*"

Mrs. Davies entered the room, concerned. "Kara, honey, what's wrong?"

"Mom, I can't find the Bisou sweater, the new pink one we bought!"

"I'm sure it's here somewhere. Did you look in the—" Mrs. Davies turned to stare at the empty closet.

"Whoa! Looks like The Gap exploded in here." Kyle, Kara's one-year-older brother, walked in, waving an ice-cream bar.

Kara whirled on him. "Kyle, did you take my new sweater?"

"Get real," Kyle laughed.

"I'll look downstairs, hon," Mrs. Davies said. "You'd better start cleaning up," she added on her way out.

"Hi, Kyle," said Tiffany from the phone speaker.

"Hi yourself."

"Kyle! If you drip anything in here, you're a memory!"

"Kara, here's the fax from the town council." Her father, the mayor of their town, walked in, casually dressed in running pants and a sweatshirt.

"Dad! I have a *real* crisis! I can't deal with that right now."

Mayor Davies gingerly stepped over some stuffed animals, victims of the fashion fallout. "It's the information for the Ravenswood Preserve website."

Kara groaned. Ever since she'd convinced her dad to let her and those girls she'd met a few weeks ago, Emily and Adriane, launch the Ravenswood Wildlife Preservation Society, she'd been regretting it. Together, the girls had convinced the town council that the old wildlife preserve was safe from dangerous animals, and that reopening it could benefit the town. They had even promised to set up an info-packed website all about conservation and endangered animals. Sure, it had seemed important at the time, but that was then. This was now, and now Kara needed to get ready. This was *seventh* grade.

"I'm sure you and your friends will want to get going on this," her father continued. "And you've got to *please* keep Mrs. Windor off my back. She's still lobbying to turn the preserve into a country club, so if you want to keep Ravenswood, give me something."

beachbunny: What's going on at Ravenswood?
goodgollymoll: Kara's gonna be protecting purple bears with her new friends
credhed: what new friends? :(

Tiffany, Heather, and Molly were her buds, but she could hardly tell them why she was part of the Ravenswood team. Not even her own dear daddy *really* knew why she had to get along with Adriane Charday and Emily Fletcher. And, if she told any of them, they would never believe her.

A new IM chirped on the computer screen outside the chatroom.

docdolittle: Hey Kara, whats up?

Kara glanced at the IM and nudged Kyle aside, flicking her fingers over the keypad.

kstar: what
docdolittle: did you get the info on the council website :)
kstar: Ya, but I'm busy with my friends now, g2g

Kara closed out Emily's IM. Her friends (her *real*

friends that she'd known since *forever*, she reminded herself) were waiting.

"What about the missing sweater?" Tiff asked over the phone.

"I'll think of something. Oh, and don't forget the barbecue here Saturday."

"Cool. Okay, see you tomorrow." There was a loud click from the speakerphone as Tiffany hung up.

beachbunny: l8rz
credhed: cu k
goodgollymolly: Good luck :)

"All right, *out*!" she ordered Kyle.

"Marcus and Joey are coming over Saturday, too," Kyle managed to get in before being pushed out the door.

"No way! Girls' night only! *Dad!*"

The mayor shrugged his shoulders. "Just remember, the Ravenswood project was your idea, Princess, so I'm counting on you."

"Okay, Daddy." Kara pouted as the door closed, then turned and kicked a pile of clothes into her closet. She was starting to hate Ravenswood. It was supposed to be a chance for her to shine (to host fund-raising parties and lead tours through amazing gardens—not *work*! But what she really hated was walking around with that big secret she had spent the last few weeks *not* blabbing about.

Magic.

Genuine magic that only the three of them could work. Well, just Adriane and Emily. They had found the most awesome gemstones that controlled the magic.

Emily had healed sick animals and Adriane had done all kinds of tricks and made friends with a magical wolf named Stormbringer. Kara didn't have her own jewel, but every time she got near their stones, the magic got stronger, as if she were supercharged. Just think what will happen when I get my own magic jewel! Kara smiled. She deserved to have the best jewel and the best magic. Maybe she'd even find the best magical animal, too. After all, that was what they were really doing at Ravenswood—helping magical animals.

Kara sighed and focused on the task at hand: clean up. She'd have to settle for option two for her first-day-of-school outfit. The lost sweater would turn up somewhere.

2

*T*HE UNICORN STOOD *in the woodland meadow. His deep golden eyes were wary but unafraid. Wildflowers blanketed the field in bright colors as Kara walked toward the magnificent creature. The unicorn raised his glimmering crystal horn, filling the meadow with flashes of brilliant light.*

Kara circled the great creature. He was breathtakingly beautiful. She ran a hand over his lustrous white hide; it felt soft as silk and shimmered gently. Breathing slowly, the unicorn lowered his head as Kara came around to look into his eyes.

His voice suddenly filled her head.

"I am for the blazing star."

She was special. If anyone were to ride a unicorn, of course it would be her.

With a leap, she was on his back.

The unicorn took off, racing across the open field. Confident, Kara leaned forward into the creature's steady gallop, feeling herself one with the animal, just as she had been taught at riding school. But this was no ordinary animal. This was the most magical of all creatures. The unicorn raced through the meadow and leaped. Instantly a portal opened—a circle of swirling stars hanging in the air before them—and the unicorn swept through.

Kara was bathed in diamond light as endless loops woven together in intricate patterns revealed itself before her: the magic web that connected worlds. Together Kara and the unicorn ran, faster . . . faster . . . streaking across the infinite web of magic.

"Come to me . . ." *Another voice, distant yet commanding, cut through her mind like steel.*

The unicorn raced along the web like white fire.

She was a golden girl, adored by all. She was a goddess, born to be with such a magnificent creature.

"You will be mine . . ."

She was a princess of magic . . . No! She was a . . . queen!

" . . . or everything you love will die!"

The unicorn stumbled. Kara flew headlong, golden hair tangling as she tossed and turned. A dark-robed figure watched, indifferent, as Kara fell, a shooting star fading into darkness.

Kara's eyes sprang open. It was pitch-black. Her heart pounded. For a second she couldn't move, then realized she was completely tangled in her bed sheets. She wriggled and kicked them off, ripping her pink satin sleep mask from her eyes.

At first she thought that the cold had awakened her, since the hairs along her arms and the back of her neck were standing up. But the room was humid, too warm for comfort. Blearily, she pushed her hair out of her face and looked around.

Pale moonlight glazed the room, glowing softly through the curtains as they wavered in the breeze. The air-conditioning must have gone out, she thought, burrowing back into her pillow. But then there wouldn't be a breeze, would there? As her brain fought its way to sense, she sat up.

The far window was wide open.

Puzzled, Kara stumbled over to shut the window. Had she forgotten before? She'd been pretty tired . . . She stopped short. The window screen was gone. She peered out into the darkness, but nothing moved, no sound broke the stillness. The screen must have fallen off some-how, she thought. Then she saw something on the ledge below her window: splotches of glowing, green muck, dripping into the gutter.

That's disgusting! How dare some big bird drop a surprise on their roof!

She closed the window with a bang and locked it. Shaken, she climbed back into bed, adjusted her sleep mask, and went back to sleep.

In the dark, beyond the window, two piercing green eyes stared back at her, then winked out.

3

FACT OF LIFE: Some people complain about school. Go figure.

Not Kara. School was the best place to wear the newest clothes, catch the latest buzz, and see all her buds. Schoolwork was like a game—and she wasn't bad at it. Not that she was a brainiac—not her style at all. She was a people person and knew how to use that skill to her best advantage. Nobody expected her to be an A student, and with everybody ready to help her if she needed it, what could be easier?

"Who'd you get for homeroom?" Molly shouted over the chaos in the hallway, brushing her dark hair as kids swirled around them, looking for lockers and classrooms.

"Heather and I got Mrs. Fitch, can you believe it?" Kara beamed.

"Oooh, you're so lucky! I got Ms. Scalise."

"See you at lunch—and, nice dress," Kara told Molly.

"You like it? Thanks." Molly looked grateful. "You look excellent, as usual. Hey, you find that sweater?"

"Not yet, it's a mystery." Kara flashed on the glowing green slime. But that was too spooky. She was in the real world now, her world. She tucked her white linen shirt more securely into her aqua-blue capris.

Smiling, Kara sauntered over to her new locker. Opening her backpack, she set up her command post. She positioned a mirror at eye level and a stickup light above, hung a brush from the side hook, and pasted an air freshener up in the top compartment. Books got stashed where they wouldn't get in the way.

"Perfect!" she said, slinging the backpack with her laptop and supplies over her shoulder.

Heather came flouncing down the hall. "Kara, come on! Everything okay?"

Kara nodded approvingly at the way Heather's white cashmere sweater complemented her long red hair. "Let's go."

Homeroom was a sunny classroom on the second floor. Kara picked a desk by the window. Heather sat right behind her, easy for Kara to swing around and chat.

Mrs. Fitch welcomed everyone and droned on about class assignments and homework. Kara's gaze kept wandering out the window. She had been so busy getting ready this morning, she'd forgotten to mention the missing screen to her father. *Glowing, green, dripping* . . . Thoughts of what had happened to her just a few weeks ago tumbled through her mind. At Ravenswood Preserve, creatures not of this world had arrived through a magical doorway—a portal. Some were cute, like the talking ferret named Ozzie. Some were mysterious, like the giant wolf, Storm, who could evaporate into mist. Some were dangerous, horrible, and scary, like the manticore that had terrorized the town for weeks. She tried to block those images and concentrate on where she was, in the real world, but she knew *they* were real, also. As real as the "purple bear," Phel. Everyone thought the bear had escaped, but she knew better. She, Emily, and Adriane had helped the creature return home—wherever that was. She also knew it wasn't really a bear—it was magic, just like the jewels Adriane and Emily found, jewels she didn't have . . . yet! They had used magic to open the portal, and Phel had gone home. She imagined herself leaping through the portal atop the most beautiful magical animal of all: a snow-white unicorn with a diamond-bright, sparkly horn. Riding together along stands of gold, friends forever. But that was a dream. Something had torn away her screen, and that was real. What if another monster had come to Ravenswood again? She felt goose bumps shiver over her shoulders.

Something moved outside the window. Just twenty

feet away, a huge animal was half hidden in the branches of a maple tree. Kara froze. Suddenly she felt a connection, almost like an electrical shock, as if this creature knew her, knew she would be right here, right now. It turned its head. Cold green eyes zeroed in on her.

Someone screamed.

Kara looked around and realized it was her. The classroom was silent. Surprised faces were staring at her.

This can't be happening!

Heather's mouth hung open in a shocked grin; others were snickering.

"Miss Davies? Is everything all right?" Mrs. Fitch looked concerned.

Kara pointed to the tree outside the window. "That big cat," she said meekly. "It's staring at me."

Half the class got up and ran to the window to look. Mrs. Fitch looked out also, but there was nothing there.

"I don't see a cat," the teacher said.

"Maybe it's the *purple bear*," someone mocked.

The room exploded in laughter.

Kara felt her ears burning.

"All right! That's enough. There's nothing more to see. Take your seats. You, too, Miss Davies."

Kara hunkered down in her seat, fuming at the snickers and stares.

"That was, like, *so* weird!" Heather whispered behind her as Mrs. Fitch handed out a sheaf of papers to pass to the back.

Kara felt shaken and frightened. There had been a cat, but how could any cat be that big? What was it doing in the tree? Was it following her? What could it want? She tried to get a grip, but only thought of one thing: Ravenswood.

∞

THE REST OF the morning went by in a blur. By the time she and Heather were cafeteria-bound, Kara felt somewhat better.

Molly and Tiffany were already waiting outside at their usual table, right under a shady tree. Carrying her tray over to them, Kara took a deep breath. Okay, chill. Maybe word hadn't spread about her bizarre disruption in homeroom.

"Been a rough morning. Kara had like a major *freakout* in homeroom," Heather announced as soon as she sat down.

"We heard," Molly said between mouthfuls of salad.

"Everyone's heard!" Tiffany added.

Guess the buzz stream's working just fine, Kara thought.

"So, what happened?" Molly asked.

"Yeah, Kara, what's up with that?" Tiffany prodded loudly.

"Quiet! Nothing. Just keep it down, you want the whole school to hear?"

"Hey, Kara, heard you saw another purple bear!" Joey Micetti stopped by the table with a tray of food, on his way to join his friends. Kara glanced around to see her brother and his buddies elbowing one another at the next table. The usual crew, Adam and . . . oh, great, that cute Marcus.

The boys were all snickering.

"This is so humiliating," Molly said, biting into her burger.

Kara sat silently.

"Go back to Pluto, Joey, with the other alien slugs!" Heather yelled.

"Maybe that's where the bear came from, outer space!" Joey taunted.

"Shows what you know. It was a big cat," Heather corrected him.

Kara wanted to disappear.

"Ooooh, a cat, that's a good one," Adam howled. "Kyle, your sister will do anything to get attention."

This day was quickly turning into a disaster. Kara was almost in tears, her face hot, mind racing. Breathe! It can't possibly get any worse.

"If she saw something, it was real!" Tiffany exclaimed.

"Suuurrre it was." Joey laughed. "Next thing you know, monsters are gonna be falling out of the sky!"

Crash!

A fur-covered thing landed in the middle of the picnic table. Food and drinks went flying. Kara and her friends screamed and jumped back as their uninvited visitor shook salad dressing off one back paw and straightened up.

"Whoa!" Joey fell over backward, startled. The other boys sprang from their table. Kids ran over to see what all the excitement was about, forming a ring around Kara's table and the creature that stood there.

4

*I*T WAS BIG, the size of a leopard. Spotted fur grew in random patches. Its body was crisscrossed with ugly scars. Dangerous eyes flashed across the crowd—and settled on Kara. She shrieked and tried to dodge behind Molly who squealed, pushed Kara away, and ran behind the tree. The big cat looked at them from under lowered brows, wild and glowering, and stalked down the table toward Kara.

Everyone panicked, yelling in confusion and excitement.

"What *is* that thing?"

"Ewwwww, it's disgusting!"

"Oh, man, that thing is wicked!"

"Someone *do* something!"

"Here, kitty, kitty." Adam was holding out his half-eaten burger, trying to lure the cat away.

"Don't feed it, you moron!" yelled Tiffany.

Kara froze, trembling, caught in the fierce glare of icy green cat eyes. Tiffany and Heather edged away from the table, but the cat didn't even glance at them. It made a noise halfway between a meow and a croak, looking right at Kara.

"Kara, run!" Tiffany cried.

But she couldn't.

The cat held Kara's gaze, its eyes searching. And suddenly Kara felt a sadness so intense she almost burst into tears.

A carton of milk splattered across the cat's back. She whirled, baring gleaming white fangs.

Joey closed in, waving a large stick. "Here, kitty!" The cat dug its front claws into the wooden table with an audible crunch. Scraggy fur stood straight up on end, making her look even bigger and scarier. The cat arched its back, bared gleaming fangs, and growled.

"Uh . . . good kitty." Joey backed off uncertainly.

The cat hissed ferociously—then lunged at him.

Joey leaped back, tripping over his own feet. "Help! Get it off!" he cried.

Gold light suddenly flared in the crowd.

"Stop it!" A tall, thin girl with long black hair stood between Joey and the cat. Adriane. Her eyes flashed with fury, daring anyone to make a move. No one did.

"Just back away," she said evenly. "She won't hurt you."

"Let me through!" Another girl pushed her way in. She had long, curly auburn hair pulled back in a ponytail. Emily. She ran right over to the animal, completely unafraid.

"Are you all right?" she asked softly, rubbing her hand gently over the cat's back, wiping away the dripping milk.

The cat looked at Emily and allowed the girl to check her over.

"Is she okay?" Adriane asked over her shoulder.

"I think so," Emily answered.

Adriane turned to Kara. "What did you do?"

Everyone stared at Kara.

"It's that creepy girl who lives in the woods, Adriane something," Kara heard Tiffany tell Heather.

"The other one is Emily Fletcher," Heather responded. "Her mom's the vet."

Kara gaped in disbelief. This was too much. How dare Adriane take that tone with her! Right in front of everybody!

Blue light sparkled as Emily's bracelet slid down to her wrist. Quickly she shoved her hand into her pocket, hiding her rainbow gemstone. "It's okay, Adriane," Emily said. She explained to everyone, "The cat lives at Ravenswood Preserve."

"What's it doing here?" Molly called out.

"It could bite somebody!" Kyle added.

Joey pushed forward. "Look at it. It's got rabies or something."

"She does not have rabies and you stay away from her!" Adriane was instantly in his face, fists balling at her sides.

Joey stepped back, embarrassed.

Kara noticed the tigereye gem at Adriane's wrist pulsing with gold light.

Adriane looked at Kara, then at her bracelet, and backed away. "She must have wandered down here, that's all."

"And Kara found her," Emily added.

"I didn't find your cat, it found me," Kara firmly told Emily.

Emily eyed Kara with interest.

"Ahh!" Molly shrieked and ran behind Kara. "It's in the tree!"

While they'd been arguing, the cat had leaped from the picnic table up into the big tree. Nimbly leaping from branch to branch, she found a way into the next tree, over the school fence, and into the woods beyond. Emily called after her, but the cat had disappeared.

As kids returned to their tables, Emily turned to Kara. "We have work to do this weekend."

Tiffany, Heather, and Molly shot Kara a look.

Emily noticed and quickly added, "We're setting up the Ravenswood Wildlife Preservation Society. It's like an independent school project."

"Kara, you're going to be working with *them*?" Molly asked, right in front of Emily and Adriane.

"In the woods?" Tiffany added, her face contorted in disgust.

"I can't believe you'd want to have anything to do with that," Heather scoffed.

"Well, it was all Kara's idea, actually. She's president," Adriane informed them with a smirk.

The girls all looked at Kara again. She gave Adriane a fierce glower, but she really felt like diving under the table.

Luckily the bell rang for afternoon classes. As kids hustled their trays to the disposal stations, the buzz was loud and clear: this was the coolest first day of school *ever*!

"We'll see you on Saturday," Emily said as they started to head back inside.

"I thought you were seeing *us* Saturday," Molly pouted. "Shopping and then the barbecue."

Kara hushed her friend, but she saw that Emily had heard. "Look, I promised my dad I would . . . look after things for him."

"It's so creepy!" Tiffany exclaimed.

"I'll be back in plenty of time for the barbecue," Kara assured them. "Just come over at six."

Kara led Molly inside. She sensed Heather and Tiffany softly whispering behind her back. Her ears burned.

This was not going at all like she had planned. How could she tell her friends what was really going on at

Ravenswood? If they only knew how incredible those jewels were, what you could *do* with them. She sighed. At least she didn't look like a complete lunatic—the cat was real. But why was it stalking her? She hoped all this weirdness was over, but she had a bad feeling it was just getting started.

5

O N SATURDAY, THE air tingled with the scent of
pine and moss as Kara walked up the road that
led to Ravenswood Preserve.

Heather, Tiffany, and Molly had made it clear they
totally disapproved of her plans to work with Emily and
Adriane. Kara felt irritated. How'd she end up in the
middle of her best friends and . . . well . . . *them*?

Okay, so Emily and Adriane were the only other two
human beings on Earth who knew that the magic was
real. But at school, they were so . . . unpopular. Hanging
with them could make *her* unpopular as well—right? Yet
the adventure they had shared still played across her
mind, a fairy tale with magic and magical creatures.

Well, there's room for only one princess in this fairy tale. If she was going to be president of the Ravenswood Wildlife Preservation Society, she would have to get her own magic jewel—and soon! She'd make it up to Moll, Tiff, and Heather tonight.

Emily and Adriane were waiting for her as she approached the twin iron gates of the Ravenswood Preserve entrance.

"How are you doing, Kara?" Emily asked.

"Terrific," Kara answered sarcastically.

The tall gates creaked as Adriane pushed them open.

"So, what do we do first?" Kara adjusted her leather backpack and followed them up the gravel road.

"Adriane's gran said there's a computer in the library," Emily explained. "We thought we'd see if we can find it. We know the preserve used to have a website."

"Fine," Kara answered. "Let's just do this. I have a party to get ready for."

"We wouldn't want to keep you from your *friends*." Adriane tossed her long black hair over her shoulder and glared at Kara. Kara glared back as the girls made their way toward the manor house. The woods were quiet and peaceful in the warm afternoon sunlight. That lasted about three seconds.

"You should've told us right away the cat was on school grounds!" Adriane said angrily.

"Oh, now I'm supposed to report to you?" Kara was really getting annoyed. "Who put you in charge, anyway?"

"You gonna turn around and have the cat hunted down, too?"

Kara stopped and crossed her arms.

Emily quickly inserted herself between the two. "Adriane, Kara didn't know Phel wasn't a monster."

"Don't take her side, you always do that!" Adriane accused Emily.

Kara was fuming. "You got the preserve back! You and *Gran* have a place to live, as quaint as that is. What is your problem?"

"You are!" Adriane didn't skip a beat. "We don't hear anything from you for two weeks and then you waltz right in as if nothing has happened."

"So what? I've been busy."

"But something *has* happened, hasn't it, Kara?" Emily asked softly.

Kara shook her head. "Look, let's just get the site online so I can tell my dad it's done, and you can go play all you want with your—"

Adriane narrowed her eyes. "Our what?"

"Never mind," Kara said, turning away behind her curtain of golden hair.

"Go ahead, let's get this out." Adriane moved around to face Kara. "You can't stand the fact that we have magic jewels and you don't!"

"Adriane—" Emily touched her friend's arm.

"No!" Adriane continued, shaking Emily's hand off. "I don't have to take this attitude from Miss Perfect, with her perfect clothes and her perfect friends!"

"Now that you mention it, I *don't* have a jewel," Kara shot back. "I have school now, and . . . things to do."

"So do we!" Adriane stepped back and assumed a fighting stance. Kara tensed.

Adriane spun in a balanced martial arts move. She swung her arm and a ribbon of golden light spiraled from the tigereye gem at her wrist. She whipped the stream of light into a golden ring. The dark-haired girl gracefully moved her arms, and the ring settled around Kara. Adriane resumed her stance, neat and slick. Magic sparkles danced around Kara and winked out.

Kara's mouth hung open as twinkly sparks tickled her skin.

"We've been busy, too," Adriane said, and turned away to continue down the road.

A cloud of mist swirled out from between the trees. The mist seemed to fold in on itself and grow darker, then vanished as Stormbringer appeared. The great silver-gray wolf padded over to Kara.

"We've been waiting for you, Kara."

The sound of the wolf's voice in her head was startling. "You . . . you have?" Kara looked into gentle, golden wolf eyes.

"The animals want to thank you for securing this home."

"They do?" Kara asked, looking at Emily.

"They're all anxious to see you, Kara," Emily told her.

"They are?" Kara looked at Adriane.

Adriane gave Kara a curt nod.

"We've also mapped a tour route of the preserve for you to show your dad and the town council," Emily said.

"Our *special* animal friends will hide in the glade when the tours are scheduled," Adriane continued.

"Wait till you see, Kara, it's so cool!" Emily's eyes sparkled.

Suddenly Kara felt as if she'd been left behind. What had happened here in the two weeks since she convinced her father to let the girls work at the preserve?

They rounded a bend and entered the grand circular driveway in front of Ravenswood Manor. With its towers and stained glass, the amazing old building looked like a castle. Ivy crawled up the stone walls to reach gargoyles perched under the eaves. Kara thought it looked haunted.

"What about the manor?" she asked. "Will that be part of the tour?"

"We haven't explored much of it yet," Emily responded.

"The garden tours and website should keep the council off our backs till we figure out how much of the manor we want to include," Adriane added.

Kara was actually starting to get excited. Emily and Adriane were really taking this seriously.

"Come on." Emily laughed as she walked around the cobblestone path that skirted the manor. "Ozzie's with the animals out back."

Kara and Adriane followed, glaring at each other.

"Show-off!"

"Barbie!"

"Come on, hurry!" Emily shouted, running out onto the manicured sea of grass that was the great lawn behind the manor. Kara was surprised by a cacophony of neighing, bleating, hooting, and other less identifiable sounds. Before her stood a herd of animals.

"All right, everyone. Calm down." A gold-and-brown ferret paced back and forth in front of the crowd like a small furry general.

The animals surged forward, bounding over the ferret.

"GaHoonk!" came his muffled response.

Incredible animals surrounded Kara; butterfly-winged horses, green-and-purple-striped deer with long, floppy ears, silver duck-like things, and others even more outrageous. Kara felt giddy.

"I am Ronif," one of the silver duck-things announced—quiffles, Emily had said they were called. "Emily and Adriane told us how you helped to give us a home here."

"Stories will be passed down to generations of quiffles," another quiffle proclaimed.

"The town allowed the preserve to stay open," Kara said modestly. "I really didn't do much."

"You helped fight off the manticore!" a winged pony said.

The animals cheered.

The ferret came bounding over. "Welcome back, Kara.

Your friends missed you."

"I don't know about that, Ozzie," Kara said, bending down to speak to him. "Things seem to be going fine here without me."

"Nonsense. It's been much too boring." The ferret smiled.

Kara grinned, though she was a little embarrassed to be talking to a ferret. Well, not really a ferret, she reminded herself—he claimed to be an elf trapped in a ferret body, but Kara had her doubts. Would an embattled world of magic really send a *ferret* to find help against the forces of evil?

Emily stepped forward. "Okay, everyone, roll call!"

With quacks, neighs, and a hoot, the animals quickly fell into a line, shoulder to shoulder across the lawn. A large, white snow owl glided gracefully out of the sky to land on Emily's arm. Turquoise and lavender glistened in her wing feathers.

"I'm here."

"Thank you, Ariel," Emily said. "You remember Ariel," she said to Kara.

Kara gave the magnificent owl a little wave.

Emily took out a notebook and began to check off her list. "Pegasi?"

"We're here," a winged pony announced.

"Thank you, Balthazar. We have four pegasi," she said so seriously that Kara almost laughed.

"Quiffles?"

"All here," Ronif announced. Adriane scooped up four baby quiffles, and immediately the other little ones tried to leap up into her arms. She fell over in the grass laughing, covered in quiffle kisses.

"There are six adults and twelve babies." Emily checked them off, then looked around. "Where're the jeeran, Ozzie?"

"Running in the field," Ozzie said, a little annoyed. "They can't stand still for more than two minutes!"

Kara looked across the lawn and saw the tail end of a green-and-purple-striped deer soaring over a hedge.

"We also have seventeen jeeran," Emily commented proudly, as if she were talking about normal deer, not some magical creatures from another world! She looked back at her list. "Brimbees?" she called out briskly.

"Here!" came a light, breathy voice.

Kara stared at what looked like big blue rabbits with iridescent dark blue spots.

Emily nodded. "Okay, that's everyone."

A small golden-winged creature about the size of a bat zipped up between the brimbees and hovered. It gave a squeak, its jeweled eyes dancing brightly.

"Who are you?" Emily asked, looking over her list.

"Skookee!" The bird-thing buzzed around Kara's head, picking at her long hair.

"Hey!" Kara ducked, swatting it away.

Ariel eyed the little flier with a hungry hoot.

The gold bird-thing gave a loud squawk, zipped off,

and vanished.

"What was that?" Kara asked, brushing her hair back into place.

"I don't know." Emily re-checked her call sheet. "Anyone come through this morning?"

"Not on my watch!" Ozzie answered stoutly.

"Ozzie, this is a sanctuary," Adriane reminded him.

A large shape slunk behind the pegasi. Kara caught the glint of green eyes.

The big cat watched her, casually turned, and walked away.

"And, of course, the cat," Emily said. "She comes and goes, but she sure seems to be interested in you," Emily commented.

"I'll say!" Kara blurted out. "The school's going to be talking about it for weeks!"

"Yeah, so will the town council," Adriane said, depositing the baby quiffles back with the adults. "Including that horrible Mrs. Windor," she added with a shudder. "She's been against Ravenswood from the start. If she hears about a wild animal showing up at school, our wildlife preserve, and my home, are as good as gone."

6

KARA FOLLOWED THE other girls through a back door into the manor. Inside, a short set of steps led to the first floor. Wide hallways lined with paintings opened onto bright sitting rooms filled with plush furniture.

"Wait till you see the library, come on!" Emily said, as she propelled Kara up a steep staircase, down a hallway, and into a room straight out of the nineteenth century.

"Wow!" Kara breathed.

They were inside a gigantic round library, illuminated in golden radiance. Kara stared up at a vast domed ceiling. Zodiac figures with twinkling stars inset were painted on it in fine gold. Below the dome hung a complicated mobile of suns and planets, shiny discs of metal

on long arms. Large oval windows overlooked the great lawn and beautiful gardens out back. Across the parquet floor, a ladder was mounted on a track that ran around the perimeter of the room, allowing access to shelves high above. Books were crammed everywhere.

Kara walked over to look at a drawing taped to the wall. It was a map of the preserve. All of the gardens were noted, and dotted lines crisscrossed the area, carefully avoiding the special glade that lay hidden behind the ancient monument known as the Rocking Stone.

"Why does that garden have an X on it?" Kara asked, pointing to a section of the map.

"Some of the gardens are overgrown since we can't maintain everything ourselves," Adriane replied. "That one is the hedge maze. Gran said you can get lost in there for days, so it's off-limits for tours."

"Well, this library alone is worth a tour," Kara said, turning around to take in the amazing room.

"No way," Adriane countered. "We don't know what special stuff is hidden in here."

Kara shrugged. "Fine, let's just get the website online."

"I've been working on some ideas on how to organize it." Emily indicated the notebooks lying open on the desk.

"I can get Kyle and Joey to set something up," Kara said, looking over Emily's papers. "They live for this stuff."

"Are you nuts?" Adriane burst out. "We're not bringing those loudmouths in here. We can figure it out ourselves."

"Okaaay, if you say so," Kara said. "How about a blog?"

"We can't go blogging this all over the place," Adriane argued. "A website is more secure."

"The original website went down two years ago," Emily said.

"Just about when Mr. Gardener disappeared," Adriane noted.

Henry Gardener, the owner of Ravenswood, had mysteriously vanished, leaving the preserve under the care of Adriane's grandmother.

"It would be a lot easier if we could find Mr. Gardener's computer," Emily continued. "Maybe we can use his files to set up the site."

"Probably buried under all this stuff." Kara gestured at globes, telescopes, dragon-shaped chess pieces and compasses littering a wide mahogany table.

"Let's see the instructions from the council."

"Here." Kara opened her backpack and handed the fax to Emily.

"We should list all the animals: numbers, physical descriptions, habits and habitats, patterns—"

"Oh, really? You gonna add dwimbees?" Kara asked.

"Brimbees," Emily corrected.

"Yeah, those, too."

"Let's check for wi-fi," Adriane suggested.

"With what?" Kara asked, waving her arms around. "I don't see a computer here, do you?"

Adriane and Emily looked at her.

"What? Oh, no! You're not using my laptop."

"Come on, Kara, just to get us started," Emily said.

"I see how it works," Kara huffed. "You only want me for my stuff. Fine!" She pulled the pink laptop out of her backpack and opened it.

Emily booted up, opened the browser, and typed the town council's web address. "We have a connection."

The computer whirred, buzzed . . . and crashed.

"Great!" Kara yelled.

"That's strange," Emily mused as she rebooted. "We lost the council server."

"The line live?" Adriane asked.

An IM pinged onscreen.

beachbunny: Hey kstar—dance class was awesome :0) can't believe u missed it

goodgollymolly: Kstar who's gone be at the bbq? :)

Kara pushed past Emily's shoulder and flicked her fingers across the keypad.

kstar: not home, still working, just be there at 6

beachbunny: not home? U still at that creepy preserve with those creepy girls?

Kara felt her face flush.

kstar: g2g l8rz

She turned off the IMs.

"Thanks for giving up your precious time for us *creeps!*" Adriane seethed behind her.

"I didn't say that," Kara said meekly, stepping away.

"You can't judge Kara by her friends," Emily chided.

"She may be your friend, but she's not mine!" Adriane glared.

Kara was shocked.

"Kara, Adriane didn't mean that," Emily said.

"There wouldn't even *be* a club without me," Kara burst out.

"This is not a club!" Adriane yelled back.

Kara pressed on. "You like the fact that you have a magic jewel and I don't. And if I never find one, that would suit you just fine, wouldn't it?"

"Nobody's trying to keep you from finding a stone," Emily assured her.

"You want my stuff, fine. But don't expect me to stand around and be insulted." With that she turned and stormed to the far side of the room.

"Give her some space," Emily said, turning back to the laptop.

"I'd like to give her outer space," Adriane replied.

Kara pushed through the door, slammed it behind her, and stomped down the stairs. How dare they treat her that way? Especially when she was giving up a Saturday with her friends to be with them!

A feeling of righteous indignation swept over her as she walked outside and crossed the stone terrace behind the manor. She stopped to look up at the library windows, checking to see if Emily and Adriane were watching. But the big oval windows only reflected the sunny sky.

"They can keep their magical stuff," she grumbled. "Magic doesn't like me anyway!"

Kara marched straight across the lawn toward a row of giant hedges. She didn't notice the swarm of colorful creatures diving from the skies to follow her.

7

*B*EING OUTSIDE HELPED clear her head. Kara took a deep breath and looked back at the expanse of the great lawn. What a perfect place for the first fund-raising event. Now *that* was something she could handle! She imagined medieval torches encircling the magnificent gardens with the rocking sounds of Sampleton Malls blasting from the stage! She giggled. And Kara, the princess of the ball, in the most rad leather-and-silk gown, dancing the night away with the most handsome prince. Adriane can stay home and be the wicked stepsister she thought with a laugh and twirled past the rose gardens.

Such beautiful roses. She bent to admire a striking patch of China reds and rugosas. An amazing flower caught her eye. It looked like a dandelion, except the seeds were bright rainbow sparkles. It reminded her of Emily's magic jewel. *Zip!* Something buzzed past her ear.

"Koook."

"Hey! Watch it!" It was one of those bird-things, a blue one. Up close it didn't look like a bird, it looked more like a . . . a . . . tiny dragon! It hovered above the rainbow flower, dipped its small front paws in the seeds, and grabbed them. With a squeak it flew away, trailing rainbow sparkles behind it. Kara stood still as another one came out of nowhere. It hovered in front of her. This one was purple. It definitely looked like a miniature flying dragon, with jeweled eyes that reflected glints of light. A dragon . . . fly. Kara was pleased with the wordplay. A dragonfly!

"Scrook?"

"Shoo," Kara replied.

"Screeek!" The purple dragonfly swirled around Kara's head, picking at her hair. Kara waved it away, and it zipped over to another flower, grabbed clawfuls of seeds, and took off.

Kara was curious. Why were the little dragons taking the seeds? To spread them somewhere else? Bet Emily and Adriane don't know about his, she thought gleefully. She looked at her watch: 4:00. Time to collect her stuff and head home. Her friends were coming over at six.

She turned to go back to the manor, but the roses and brambles seemed to have gotten all tangled up behind her. She tried to push through. Ouch! The thorns were sharp.

Kara cut through an opening in the hedges and started down an overgrown path walled in on either side by towering hedgerows.

The path came to a dead end at the head of a T: she could go right or left. It looked like some kind of giant maze, she realized. *Gran said you could get lost in the hedge maze for days, so it's off-limits for tours . . .* Yeah, right, who would be so stupid to . . . well, getting lost in a hedge maze was just stupid.

Kara looked around. The hedgerows loomed above her, blocking the view of the manor.

"Hey! Hello? Ozzie? Storm? Someone? I'm . . . lost!" Where were all the animals now that she needed help? She kicked her sneaker along the gravel and a small cloud of rainbow seeds sparkled up into the air. Probably dropped by those pesky dragonflies. The cloud of seeds trailed to the right, so Kara followed. She walked into a wide circle with trails leading off in at least a dozen different directions.

There was a soft rustle in the hedge. She caught a glimpse of an animal rounding a corner.

"Hey, Dwimbee!" Kara ran around the corner and gasped. The big cat sat in the middle of the path, her green eyes gazing at Kara.

The cat yawned, then stood and strolled deeper into the maze, glancing over her shoulder.

She expected Kara to follow?! How dumb did that cat think she was?

The cat turned and blinked at her.

"I'm coming, keep your fur on!" Kara grumbled and crunched along, dire thoughts of rock'n'roll princesses who wander away from the party and get lost forever in enchanted hedgerows playing in her head.

The cat moved purposefully through the twisting green corridors.

Then she turned a corner—and walked out of the maze.

"Thank goodness! I thought we were going to be stuck in there forever!"

The cat was threading her way into a patch of deep woods.

"Hey, kitty! Wait for me." She set off into the trees, hurrying to keep the cat in sight. Deep, dense forest now surrounded her. But at least she was on a path, muddy and narrow, but definitely a trail.

"Kitty, where are you?" she called.

She saw the cat entering a wall of giant firs. Kara scrambled after her, looking up in awe at the trees, their green boughs covering the sky. She emerged into a wide-open clearing in the woods. A stream bubbled by, running into a large pond. Fir trees circled the glade protectively, and on the far side, the immense boulder called the Rocking Stone stretched its rocky finger way up into the skies.

Finally, a landmark she recognized! Beyond the Rocking Stone was a path that would take her back to the manor house. It was a moment before she realized where she really was—at the *secret* glade, where Emily had found her magic healing stone.

Kara headed for the pond. There, in the shade of weeping willow trees, something sparkled in the crystal-clear water. She knelt down to look closer. Stones, dozens of beautiful stones! She reached into the water and scooped up a handful; they were rough and unpolished, but flecked with crystal. Woot! A ton of *magic stones*! She held up a tiny green one and closed her eyes, concentrating on making the stone light up the way Emily's and Adriane's could. Nothing happened. She tossed it away and tried again with a yellow one, then a blue one. Nothing.

These didn't feel magical at all! Then again, how do you know if a stone is magical or not? The feeling that maybe she just didn't have what it took to make magic came over her. She had helped Adriane and Emily with magic, but the key word was "helped."

She looked up to see the cat sitting next to her. The animal's green eyes were magnetic, filled with deep empathy. Once again, Kara was shaken by the intensity of the feeling. The cat nodded toward a rock by the edge of the water. Kara scampered over and looked behind it.

Half submerged in the shallows was the most beautiful crystal Kara had ever seen. It was teardrop-shaped and scalloped like an ornate shell. She reached down and picked it up. Smooth and polished, it gleamed diamond bright, reflecting light in all directions. She stood up and held the stone tight.

Instantly, warmth pulsed up Kara's arm! It seemed to lodge in her heart and her eyes and her brain. The gem flashed, sending rainbows around the clearing. Magic! Kara jumped for sheer joy, shrieking with the wonder of it. She waved her arm in a circle and brilliant twinkles spiraled from the gem.

"I can't believe it," she cried. A magic jewel! A stone, her own stone, and the most beautiful one of all!

She danced over to the cat. "Thank you, thank you so much!"

It was as if she'd turned on a faucet of magic. Multicolored bubbles streamed everywhere, popping and bouncing around her. Kara spun in a circle, stretching her arms out, trailing ribbons of light from her jewel.

"Look at meeeeee!" she sang. "I have magic!"

"Sreeeeeeep!"

"Whoooooohoooo!" Kara cried.

"WOooOOooh . . ."

"Yeeheep!"

"Yeah, that's meeee—"

"Keekeee!"

Kara whirled to a stop. Wait a minute!

Five dragonflies were singing and dancing with her, ecstatically whirling and twirling in the air. Dozens more rocketed about, bursting out of bubbles of color. They thronged around her, chirping and flashing!

This was magic and it was better than she could ever have imagined. No wonder Emily and Adriane were so in love with it!

"Can you believe this? The others'll absolutely die!" Adriane's tigereye and Emily's rainbow jewel were cool, but just wait until they saw *this* stone!

"It makes an impressive display."

"Oh, doesn't it? I can feel it, it's the most mag . . . gi . . . cal . . ." Kara slowly turned back to the cat. "What?"

"It suits you."

A look of suspicion crossed Kara's face. "You can talk?"

"Most humans have a hard time hearing without some magical assistance," the cat told her. She began to groom her mottled patches of fur.

"Say that again," Kara commanded.

"I am not a trained performer," the cat said mildly, sweeping her big, rough tongue across her shoulder.

"Sorry. It's just kinda unbelievable."

A golden dragonfly settled on Kara's shoulder and grinned up at her.

"Beat it, Goldie." Kara flicked it away. It vanished in a burst of color.

"I am glad you are pleased," the cat replied, standing up.

"Oh, yes! I'm going to . . . to *magic* myself right back to the manor!"

The cat turned. *"How do you plan to accomplish that?"*

Kara blushed, then made up her mind to try. How hard could it be? She held out her gleaming stone. "Mirror, mirror . . ." No, that wouldn't work for transportation. Kara realized with surprise that she didn't have any actual idea how to work the gem. Her mind raced through possibilities. Abracadabra seemed a little risky. Twinkle, twinkle? No, that didn't seem like a good bet, either.

The cat came back a few steps. *"Start small,"* she suggested.

How did Adriane and Emily work their stones? They hadn't said anything about rhyming or spells. They just pictured something in their minds and focused on it.

Kara clutched the beautiful stone as hard as she could, squinched her eyes closed, and pictured herself rising off the ground . . .

Nothing happened.

Darn! She tried again, picturing herself as accurately as she could: lustrous blond hair, creamy skin, dewy red lips—no, she'd sworn off lip gloss long ago, make that pale pink lips—rising up, inch by inch, sparkling blue eyes still closed . . .

Her feet left the ground! She actually felt the magic pulling her into the air! She also felt little pinpricks through her shirt, along her skin, and even in her hair. She opened her eyes a crack and gasped. Dozens of little dragonflies were tugging her upward, their tiny wings beating furiously.

Her eyes flew open and she tumbled to earth—from a height of about five inches. "Hey!" Kara shouted, swatting away the pesky little things. Well, it took Adriane two weeks to figure out that trick with her stone. Just takes practice. This is going to be a blast!

"I have been watching the little dragons collecting magic seeds," the cat said. *"Those seeds compress into crystals. But the one you found doesn't feel new. It's too strong."*

"I knew it! Maybe there're more like this one," Kara said, running to the pond and searching among the pebbles in the water. The cat gave a sniff and started up the hill. "Oh, c'mon," Kara whined. But the cat kept going. "Okay, be that way."

She sat sifting through the stones as the dragonflies happily buzzed about. "Shoo, go away!"

Grabbing a few more stones, she examined them and tossed them away. The sound of gently running water echoed through the peaceful forest glen. She noticed the dragonflies had vanished. Everything was quiet except for the sounds of splashing.

Swish, swish . . .

Kara felt the oddest tingling sensation and realized the jewel was getting warm in her hand. She held it up to examine it. The stone pulsed with light, like a heartbeat. Flashes bounced off the water, sending an ashen glow into the trees beyond. The glade now seemed surreal. Suddenly she didn't feel so good. Her stomach twisted and she felt light-headed.

Swish swish . . .

There it was again. Something splashing in the water. Kara turned and saw a ragged old woman crouched by the side of the lake, dipping something into the crystal-clear water. Her face was turned away as she scrubbed in clean, swift strokes. *Swish, swish* . . . Looked like she was cleaning an article of clothing.

Was she a homeless person? What was she doing out here?

Uneasily, Kara got to her feet and approached her. The woman's whole outfit was rags, splotched and nasty. Slimy green weeds hung from her arms and legs. Yuck!

"Excuse me, are you . . . uh . . . all right?" she asked tentatively.

The ragged figure scraped the cloth up and down a rock. *Swish, swish* . . .

Kara felt dizzy. The trees were starting to sway around her. Fighting the queasiness, she looked closer. Greasy, stringy hair hung down, covering the old woman's face. Her long dress was ripped in shreds, revealing patches of pockmarked . . . *green skin!* With long, gnarly green fingers, the tattered old crone spread the cloth on the rock—it was pink.

Kara's world crumbled. Fear shot down her spine. It was her sweater! The pink sweater she had lost!

She froze, gasping for air.

The old woman turned to Kara. The . . . creature . . . had a woman's face, but its skin was green and covered

with horrible sores. Blood-red eyes were set deep at odd angles to a—there was no nose, just a ragged hole where a nose should have been. The creature's mouth twisted as a hiss escaped through thin blue lips. The mouth contorted open, the hiss building into a howl. Kara's hands flew over her ears and she screamed. The creature lurched, monstrous in her fury, clawing her way toward Kara.

8

*E*VERYTHING SEEMED TO slip into slow motion as Kara whirled around, slid on the muddy bank, and tumbled backward. One of her sneakers went flying. With dripping green claws, the ragged apparition reached for her. Something big flew at Kara and she scrambled sideways in the mud. She turned to see the cat standing between her and the ghoulish creature.

With a snarl, the cat bared fearsome fangs.

The monster howled incoherently, reaching and clawing.

Kara leaped to her feet and ran. "Ow, ow, ouch!" she shrieked as her sock-covered foot came down on sharp rocks. She gripped her gem and focused. Quick! A new pair of Nikes with shock soles! But no footwear materialized.

"Use your magic!" The cat's voice was in her head.

"I'm trying!" Kara yelled back.

Think! Do what Adriane did. Kara concentrated. Left, right, arms together, swing tight . . . She pinwheeled her arms, whipping the crystal around, and landed on one knee, jewel pointed toward the monster. Tiny sparkles fizzled from the tip. Kara frowned. That cheer routine killed at the home game.

"Kara?"

"Over that way!"

Voices were approaching from beyond the trees. A moment later the animals came charging into the glade. In the lead was Balthazar the pegasus with Ozzie standing on his back.

"What is it?" a quiffle yelled.

"Another monster!" a brimbee cried in terror as the creature lurched toward Kara.

Ozzie jumped onto the pegasus's head. "Kara, are you all right?"

"No!" Kara ran to the animals, shaking with fear. "That thing is after me!"

A cloud of swirling mist swept by and Stormbringer appeared. The great wolf bared teeth and growled low. Stormbringer and the cat closed ranks in front of Kara, blocking the advance of the creature.

Huddled in tattered rags, the horrid thing hissed, "Givesss me jewel!"

"No way!" Kara yelled. "I found it and it's mine!"

"You found a jewel?" Ozzie asked.

"Yes, look. Isn't it awesome?" She held up the crystal and felt it flare to life, sending energy prickling through her hand and up and down her arm. "It's working!" she cried.

"Quickly, gather round!" Ozzie ordered. The pegasi crowded behind Kara; brimbees and the larger quiffles pressed in close. Storm and the cat stood on each side. The jewel blazed with light.

Suddenly, dozens of colored bubbles popped above them. Dragonflies zipped out, diving and twirling. Screeching, the ragged ghoul swatted them with gnarled fingers. A bright golden dragonfly spiraled down. Piping, frantic screams cut off as it hit the water and vanished.

"Goldie!" Kara shouted in fear and anger. With her free hand she clutched the cat and the jewel exploded with fierce power.

Kara screamed as diamond fire shot straight up into the sky so unbearably bright she could see it even through her closed eyelids.

The monster hissed and backed away. Kara's arms ached as she desperately fought to control the stream of magic. It was like trying to direct a tidal wave. The stream twisted back and forth like a fiery snake, knocking Kara to the ground as it dissipated over the glade.

She opened her eyes to see a ferret face staring at her, very concerned. Other animals surrounded her.

"What happened?" Kara asked.

"Storm sensed strong magic, then we heard screaming," Ozzie said. "We followed Storm and then we clobbered the monster!"

Kara got unsteadily to her feet and realized the creature had vanished. "Wow! My magic jewel totally evaporated the monster!"

The animals had helped her, Kara realized. They had supercharged her jewel, just like she always made Emily's and Adriane's gems go crazy!

"What *was* that thing?" she asked.

"It looked like a banshee," Balthazar replied.

"A what?"

"A cursed fairy creature. But this one was worse. It was poisoned by the Black Fire."

"Well . . . what's it doing here?"

"I don't know."

Kara walked over and picked up her pink sweater. It was burned through with ragged holes. She flashed on the glowing green slime outside her bedroom window. That *thing*, that banshee had been in her room! "What was it doing with my sweater?"

"Banshees practice strange magic," Balthazar mused. "Their spells often include articles of clothing so they can track their victim."

"Victim?" Kara repeated.

She looked at the jewel, now cool in her hand. She was nobody's victim. Now she had her *own* magic jewel! Grabbing her sneaker, Kara followed the group down the trail back to the manor. She looked over her shoulder for the cat, but she was nowhere to be seen.

9

"*H*EY!" KARA BOUNDED into the library with Ozzie, the quiffles, Ronif and Rasha, and Balthazar.

Emily was examining a pile of books while Adriane rummaged through a collection of odd devices scattered about a tabletop.

Emily gasped and jumped to her feet. "What happened to you?"

Even Adriane was astonished when she turned to look at Kara.

Kara was covered in mud. Her shirt was torn, her shoelaces were undone, and her pink sneakers were caked with dirt. Her golden hair was wet, slick against her head, and full of grass and twigs.

"What do you mean?" she asked, beaming with joy.

"Are you all right?" Emily walked toward Kara, her rainbow jewel pulsing softly with turquoise light.

"Never been better." Kara rocked back and forth, arms behind her back, hiding her secret for as long as she could.

Emily looked at the animals. "What happened?"

"You should have seen it!" Ozzie blurted out.

"Seen what?" Emily asked.

"Unbelievable!" Ronif exclaimed.

"We all helped," Rasha stated.

"The cat helped, too," Kara added with a smirk. "I talked to her."

"You what?" Adriane walked over, amber light pulsing from her tigereye.

"That's right," Kara said proudly, sliding sideways under the planetarium mobile. The clockwork mechanism suddenly came to life, comets and stars revolving

and interweaving in a complex
cosmic dance. Emily's eyes
widened at the sudden move-
ment. Balthazar ducked to avoid
the swinging pendulum.

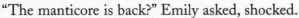

"Just what I said, I talked
to the cat—oh, and I got
attacked by a monster,"
Kara added. A comet
swung by on an arc,
following her. A shiny
planet swept by, catch-
ing Ronif and whisking
the startled quiffle into the air.

"The manticore is back?" Emily asked, shocked.

"Nooope, guess again," Kara said coyly.

"Oh, my." Ozzie stood on a table to study the intricate
mechanism of the moving mobile. He tried to grab Ronif
as the quiffle came swinging by, but a moon caught the
ferret, swinging him into orbit. "Dooooohooo!"

Adriane was losing her patience, rubbing at the pulsing stone on her wrist.
"If it wasn't the manticore, what
was it?"

"It was a homeless monster
thingy from the magic world!"
Kara declared.

"A what?"

63

"Yeah, and it was washing my pink sweater."

"Thank goodness you were there!" Adriane confirmed. "We can't have monsters running around the preserve washing clothes."

"Well, you weren't even there, Miss Kung Fu show-off," Kara gloated.

"It was a fairy creature," Balthazar said, sidestepping as Ozzie and Ronif swung by on the moving planetarium. "A banshee, but horribly mutated, poisoned by Black Fire."

"Oh, no! How did you fight it?" Emily asked.

"Hmmm, well, let me see . . . with my amazing personality? No . . . my striking good looks? No . . . my cutting-edge yet tasteful fashion sense?"

"Would you stop fooling around!" Adriane yelled.

"Maybeeeee . . . I used . . . *this!*" Kara whipped out the jewel from behind her back. It flashed like a diamond in the light, casting rainbow sparkles across the room.

Emily and Adriane stared openmouthed.

"A magic stone!" Adriane exclaimed.

"Where did you find it?" Emily asked.

"In the glade, where you found yours." Kara stopped herself from saying, and it's bigger, better—no, the *best* magic jewel ever! She swung her arm around, trailing glitter from the jewel's tip. The clockwork planetarium sped up like a carnival ride.

"Help!" Ronif and Ozzie wailed.

"Kara! That jewel activated the mobile!" Emily exclaimed.

"Stop flashing that thing around!" Adriane said, jumping up and down, trying to grab Ozzie and Ronif as they swung by.

"I'm going to turn my room pink and stick Kyle in a tree and give all my friends new iPods."

"Wise choice of magical powers," Adriane cracked as she pulled Ronif and Ozzie down.

"Kara, stop using your jewel. It's doing something to mine!" Emily held up her wrist to show her gem shifting through rainbow colors.

"Has it changed?" Adriane asked Kara.

"What do you mean?"

"I mean, both Emily's and mine were rough stones when we first found them. They became polished and even changed shape after we started using them."

Kara shrugged. "Mine doesn't have to change. It's perfect the way it is."

"It's very powerful. We all saw it," Ozzie said.

"And it could be dangerous," Emily cautioned.

"I am going to do the best magic, ever! It's too big for my wrist, sooooo . . . I'm going to make a necklace!"

"Kara, I don't think you should use it until we figure out how it works," Adriane said.

"It works great!" Kara skipped around the room, drawing shapes in the air with magic sparkles. Her jewel flared brightly, briefly outlining sections of the walls. Faint images flashed as Kara danced by, as if her magic was an X-ray machine illuminating shapes behind the oak paneling.

"There's something behind there." Adriane pointed.

Emily noticed it also. "If Mr. Gardener's computer is hidden, maybe we can find it if we all use our jewels together."

"Okeydokey." Kara liked this game, now that she was a real player.

The girls stood together in the center of the library.

Emily held up her rainbow jewel.

Adriane held up her tigereye.

Kara raised her jewel between them.

"Concentrate on a computer," Adriane said.

Blue-green and golden light flared from Emily's and Adriane's gems. They all clasped their free hands together.

Instantly the magic flowed into Kara's jewel and silver-white light burst from its tip so intensely that all three girls recoiled. The magic stream slammed into the pink laptop, launching it across the room.

Kara shrieked, dropping the other girls' hands. The magic fell away as Kara ran over to check out her laptop.

"Wrong computer," Adriane stated.

"Magic works better when we help," Balthazar offered.

The pegasus, two quiffles, and Ozzie moved in to surround the three girls.

"Okay, everyone. Let's try it again," Emily said.

Standing in the center of the library, once again the three girls clasped hands and held their jewels in the air.

The animals closed their eyes. Magic flared from Emily's and Adriane's gems and flowed into Kara's stone, sending diamond beams bouncing around the room.

The library lit up like a small city. Sections of wall glowed, revealing secret doors and hiding places, gadgets whirred and clicked, and the clockwork planets and suns zipped around their orbits.

"Concentrate on a computer!" Emily called out.

"And don't think pink," Adriane said to Kara.

Magic swirled around the room, twisting and blending into a single ribbon of turquoise, gold, and diamond-white. Suddenly the magic crashed into a section of wall, making it light up from within. A large panel slid to the side, revealing a giant screen.

"Look! Widescreen TV!" Kara exclaimed.

The golden light of the domed ceiling flashed and blinked out, casting the room in darkness except for the cool, soft glow of the screen.

"Enough!" Adriane ordered.

The girls dropped hands and let their stones cool.

Suddenly points of light, brilliant and dazzling, flashed overhead. The girls and the animals looked up in awe as a giant star map twinkled across the domed ceiling. Then they heard a voice.

"Welcome to the magic web."

10

"I T'S HIM!" EMILY gasped.

"Him who?" Kara asked.

"Mr. Gardener," Adriane said, amazed. "He owns Ravenswood. He disappeared about two years ago."

Ozzie, Ronif, Rasha, and Balthazar looked curiously at the man smiling at them from the large screen set back in the wall. He had long, gray hair and wore small, round glasses over keen blue eyes.

"What's he doing in there?" Kara wondered.

"Mr. Gardener, is that really you?" Adriane asked the image on the screen.

But no answer came. The kind face just kept smiling.

"It's a video file or something," Kara said.

Emily noticed a tray under the screen. She touched it and a keyboard slid out. "Look!"

She hit the ENTER button. The bright star map across the domed ceiling dimmed and was replaced by the golden luminescence.

"Whoever has found this station, the magic is with you," the image of Gardener announced. "I am sorry I am not here to greet you in person, for you must have many questions."

"I'll say." Kara crossed her arms.

"There is a portal, a gateway, in Ravenswood that leads to a world called Aldenmor. Sealed for centuries, it has recently opened, signaling that the time of magic has come full circle and three mages would soon be arriving."

His face faded, and the screen filled with sparkling lines like a Spirograph, lights marking various points along the grids.

Then Gardener's voice continued. "There is a web that connects many worlds, including Earth. Magic flows along this web to where it is needed. But there are very few places left that hold true magic, and over the years, the web has grown weak. If we are to save the web, we need to renew the magic from its very source, a hidden place called Avalon."

Fairimentals had come to the three girls and left them a message scrawled in the earth: Avalon. It was at the center of the whole magical mystery the girls had embarked upon.

"I have gone to seek great magic to aid you on your quest. If you are viewing this message, then I have not yet returned to begin your training. I cannot say if I have fallen to dark forces, but I can tell you this: be careful, young mages. Nary a corner of the web does not lie in some danger from a fearsome enemy. She is a magic master, twisted in her selfish desire to horde magic and use it for herself."

The image of Gardener paused, his eyes focused on them.

"This is your time, young mages. I have faith you will find what you need to fulfill your destiny. Good luck to you."

The face of Henry Gardener faded, replaced by a blank screen.

"What was that all about?" Kara asked, incredulous.

"Mr. Gardener's last message before he left," Emily ventured.

Ozzie scratched his chin. "Something is wrong. Gardener was expecting mages, not monsters."

"What exactly is a mage?" Adriane asked.

"A magic user," replied Balthazar.

"So Gardener was supposed to teach us about all this magic stuff," Kara huffed. "Thanks a lot for the help!"

"Now he's gone and he left us with nothing!" Adriane said angrily.

"What am I?" Ozzie leaped upon the keyboard. "Chopped barleycorn?"

"Of course not!" Emily kissed his furry head. "You're perfect."

"Well . . . I . . ." Ozzie swooned and sat backward upon the keys and a cursor appeared onscreen. It was a dream-catcher icon with jewels positioned top, bottom, left, and right, like the points of a compass.

"Whoa!" Ozzie scrambled to his seat as assorted icons appeared: animals, jewels, and one of Ravenswood Manor.

Emily moved the cursor around over the icons. One by one, different images of Ravenswood appeared: pictures and text about the wildlife preserve and rare animals that had lived there at one time or another.

"It must be the original Ravenswood files!" Emily exclaimed.

"Wow, so cool! Look at all this stuff on it," Adriane said.

"Good job, ferret." Kara looked at her watch. "Now how do we link it to the town council?'

Emily turned to the others. "Mr. Gardener went to a lot of trouble to keep this a secret. What if we had two sites?" she suggested. "We set up the Ravenswood Preserve site as our homepage for tour information and list the animals we *can* show on the tour, like Ariel and the other birds, Storm, peacocks, deer—but we also make a second level, our own password-encoded site."

"I like it, a secret site," Adriane said, smiling. "A web-site about magic—a magic web."

"Cute." Kara rolled her eyes. "You gonna design a space station too while you're at it?"

"Well, we can at least get our homepage up," Emily said. "But I don't think we should link it until we check out everything on here. You heard the message: we have to be careful."

"Agreed," Adriane said.

Kara frowned. "That could take . . . hours!" Again she looked at her watch: 5:30. "I'm late!" she cried. "I've got to get to my—"

The girls and animals all looked at her.

"—party," she finished sheepishly.

"So go," Adriane told her.

"Listen, Kara," Emily began. "It's okay. We know you have your friends, but we're your friends, too."

"Yeah . . ." Kara didn't look convinced.

"What I'm saying is, we share something, the three of us. Nobody else can know."

"What she's saying is, don't do anything stupid with that jewel!" Adriane cut to the chase.

"I get it." Kara was packing up her things. "No magic."

"Right. No magic until we can figure it out together. It's too dangerous," Emily said.

"Okay, I hear you!" Kara ran out the library door.

11

THE DAVIES'S LARGE Tudor house sat on meticulously landscaped grounds overlooking the Chitakaway River.

Kara raced up the driveway and burst into the kitchen with fifteen minutes to spare. A note from her mom was on the table.

"Nate and Alvin's delivery just left. Everything's ready out back. I'm meeting your father at the club. We'll be home around ten. Call us on the cell if you need us."

"Eek, I stink!" Kara took the stairs two at a time and rocketed to the bathroom for a quick shower.

A few minutes later, she dashed into her closet, scattering clothes every which way. She hopped back out, pulling on crisp new jeans and a bright green cami.

Gathering her hair back in a ponytail, she thought about what had just happened at Ravenswood—probably the most amazing thing that had ever happened to anybody on the planet! A banshee had come after her, but her animal friends had protected her. Best of all, she'd found magic.

She rummaged in her jewelry drawer and emerged with a silver chain necklace. She flipped open the locket clasp, removed the old star drops, and attached her new gem. She secured the chain around her neck.

"Perfect!"

"It is nice."

"Oh, yes," Kara agreed, looking admiringly in the mirror. "It's so . . . *what?*" She whirled around to see the enormous cat lounging among the pillows at the top of her bed. "How did you get in here?"

The cat looked coolly at Kara. *"Would've been easier if you'd left the window open."*

"You can't stay here. My mom practically freaked when I had a hamster! You're so much . . ." Kara stopped, at a loss for words. All she could think of was *worse.*

"Bigger?" A huge paw stretched, extending razor claws as a mouth full of sharp teeth yawned.

Kara nudged the cat over as she sat down to slip into a pair of slides. "Were you outside my window the other night?"

"You had another visitor as well," the cat replied.

"I can't believe that thing was in here." Kara shivered.

"I could stay and keep an eye on things, if that's okay with you."

Kara suddenly felt a little shy. "Okay with me." She ran her hand over the cat's scruffy-looking fur. "What's your name?"

"Lyra," the cat replied, eyes half closed as Kara scratched the corded muscles on her neck.

"That's pretty," Kara said, sounding surprised. "I'm Kara."

The cat yawned and lay back in the pillows.

The doorbell sounded.

Kara jumped, stopped quickly to check herself in the mirror again, then eyed Lyra. "Just stay here!" she ordered, and closed the door as she ran downstairs.

It was a perfect September evening with gentle breezes under clear skies. The table was set on the patio, overlooking a marble fountain in the garden behind the house. Candles flickered in lamps set around the yard. Tall pitchers of lemonade stood on the buffet table surrounded by plates of barbecued burgers and hot dogs, chips, salads, pickles, fruits, coleslaw, and baked beans.

Kara's friends were already in a party mood as she led them through the kitchen and into the backyard.

"Wait till we show you these rockin' routines," Tiffany told her.

Heather giggled. "You should have seen Tiff!'

"Girl, it's called rhythm, and I have got the moves!" Tiffany danced across the patio as the others laughed.

Kara smiled. Finally she could just relax and enjoy herself.

"How'd it go with you?" Molly asked.

"Yeah, tell us everything," Heather ordered, pouring some lemonade.

"Details, girl!" Tiffany shimmied by.

"Oh, you know, soooo boring." Kara twirled a strand of her blond ponytail in her fingers. "We have to research in this old library for the website."

Heather laughed. "Research?"

"Library? Sounds serious." Tiffany put her hand on Kara's forehead. "Hmm, geeky influence with a touch of dweeb," she diagnosed.

"Needs some time with her homegirls," Heather prescribed.

"And not with the beasts of the forests," Molly added, crunching into a celery stick.

"Well, there are no wild beasts around here," Kara said, firmly setting the record straight.

"Yo, yo, wass*up!*" Joey called out as Kyle and his friends spilled out onto the flagstone patio.

"Stand aside, ladies, the crew is here to bring it home," Marcus announced, placing a huge boom box on the floor.

"On second thought, I could be wrong." Kara rolled her eyes.

The girls laughed.

"Feeding time at the zoo! Let's eat!" Kyle started piling a plate with food.

"Sweet! We got some spread going on here." Joey grabbed a plate and started a first pass through the buffet.

"Hey, Kara, where are your superhero friends?" Marcus asked, filling his plate beside her.

"Huh?"

"The daring duo of the animal world!" Joey called out.

"They're not my . . . friends." Kara flushed. "I'm just working with them on the Ravenswood project for Dad."

"Joey was hoping Adriane would be here," Kyle teased.

"I was not," Joey said, his face going bright red.

"Dude, you said you like her." Kyle winked at Marcus.

"How could anyone like her?" Tiffany asked Kara. "She's so crude."

"She's okay," Kara said, more annoyed than she was willing to let on.

Tiffany stared at her as if she had grown an extra head. "What?"

"Well, Adriane only has her grandmother, and they're trying to get the preserve all fixed up."

"Exactly. *So* pathetic, right?" Tiffany said.

Kara flushed, twirling her jewel in her fingers. Adriane wasn't her friend, but the girl certainly wasn't pathetic. She was just . . . different.

"Kara, where did you get that?" Heather noticed her necklace.

"Oh, I found it . . . lying around."

Molly and Tiffany moved in to study the dazzling teardrop jewel that hung from Kara's neck.

"You always have the best accessories," Tiff said admiringly.

"It's true." Kara beamed.

"Who's for seconds?" Kyle asked, moving back to the buffet.

"The human disposal has spoken!" Kara announced. Everybody crowded around the buffet table, chattering and laughing, piling plates high.

Kara smiled. Just perfect—

"Peeep."

Something whizzed by the table and flew into the garden. It was a burger. A flying burger? Had she done that? She looked down at her jewel, but it wasn't sparkling any more than usual.

Just then a dragonfly zipped down the middle of the table, purple wings shining in the candlelight. It dodged among the plates and scooped up a couple of cherry tomatoes out of the salad bowl.

Kara's eyes bulged. Play it cool, maybe nobody will notice . . .

"Ahhhh!" screamed Heather. "What's that?"

No such luck.

"A huge flying bug!" Tiffany ducked and Molly choked. Joey leaped over to smack it away.

"Scroook!"

He smacked two tomatoes instead, splattering Tiffany and Heather.

"Hey!" Heather cried.

"Ohhh, gross!" Kyle and Marcus howled with laughter.

Okay, it's okay, Kara repeated to herself. Stay calm, everything's fine . . .

There was silence.

Everyone was looking at Kara. The girls had their mouths open. The boys were sputtering, desperately holding in their laughs.

"What?" Kara said, annoyed.

"Kara," Molly began.

"You have . . ." Tiffany continued.

Kara felt a tug on her scalp.

" . . . a big . . ." Heather stammered.

" . . . *bug* on your head!" Kyle fell over in a fit of laughter.

Something was entangled in her ponytail. Please let it be a bug, she thought. She worked her fingers through the long blond strands and something struggled frantically. "Ouch!" she yelped, as she felt a tiny stab against her scalp.

"Pweeek!"

"Kara, are you all right?" Molly asked.

"Fine, fine, it's nothing," Kara said, hopping backwards holding a fistful of hair.

She pulled a dragonfly free—a blue one.

"Skachooo!" It coughed a spark of flame and darted off into the twilight.

"Did you see that?" Molly asked, her eyes wide.

"The biggest firefly I ever saw!" Joey exclaimed. "It's like a jungle out here!"

"Kara, you sure you didn't bring your work home from the preserve?" Kyle asked.

"Very funny," Kara mumbled. "There are no wild animals around here!"

Out of the corner of her eye, she caught a large shape slinking around the buffet table. "Who wants another hot dog?" Kara grabbed a tray, quickly moving to block the view.

"I'll take one," Joey said.

Kara tossed a hot dog toward him. "What are you doing! I told you to stay put!" she whispered to Lyra, who crouched in the shadows to the side of the brick hearth.

The hot dog floated by her head. Kara reached out and grabbed it.

"Poooo!"

"Give me that!" She tugged back and forth with a red dragonfly.

"Where's my dog?" Joey asked behind her.

Kara yanked the hot dog hard and turned quickly. The dragonfly careened backward.

"Here!" She put the half eaten hot dog on Joey's plate. He walked away, puzzled.

Lyra growled low in her throat. *Something is here.*

"Thanks for the update! These dragonflies are ruining everything!"

"No, something else. It's fading in and out, fighting to stay here."

"What?" Kara looked around frantically. "Something bad?"

"No, but they've come for you." The cat slid back into the shadows.

"Hey, who's for dessert?" Kyle yelled out.

"Ice-cream sundaes, burnin'!" Joey whooped.

Is this dinner over yet? Stay calm! Everything's fine.

Drip . . .

"Hey! Something dripped on my head!" Joey said.

"Is it raining?" Tiffany asked.

Drip, drip . . .

Kara felt droplets on her face. She looked up. Not a cloud in sight.

Drip, drip, drip . . . Water was spritzing everywhere.

"Look, the fountain's screwy!" Marcus pointed.

Everyone stared at the fountain. Bursts of water were spurting from it, shooting straight into the evening air and spraying in all directions.

Kara ran across the lawn, looking around frantically.

"Web runner . . ." A tiny voice blew past like a breeze.

"Huh?" Kara looked at the tall Roman fountain, watching water spurt out over the tiered ledges. Droplets fell into the bowl like rain.

The drops swirled, shimmering as if they were trying to take shape. Kara looked closer. Twinkling and flowing, the drops merged. Kara's eyes widened. It was a tiny figure formed out of water with waves of long, crystal-blue hair. The figure shimmered, struggling to hold its form.

"The jewel . . ." The tiny figure's voice rippled across the water. Kara wasn't even sure she had heard it.

Kara leaned in closer. "What did you say?"

"Do not use the jewel . . ." The figure quivered, flowing in and out of its watery form.

"Why not?"

"It is . . . a trap."

"Kara, what are you doing?" Molly called out.

Kara whirled around and sat in the fountain, splattering the figure to droplets. "Nothing."

"You're sitting in the water!" Heather exclaimed.

The boys laughed.

"Uh, just checking the pressure. Be right there!" She jumped up and glanced back in the water. "What do you mean a trap?" she whispered.

Small geysers bubbled from the surface as two watery figures swirled to life.

"She knows you possess the jewel . . ."

"Who knows?" Kara could feel desperation from the tiny figures as they began to lose form.

"The bringer of Black Fire . . ."

"The Dark Sorceress . . ."

"Dark Sorceress? That doesn't sound good."

"Use it with care . . ."

"To your own heart be true . . ."

"Use the jewel, don't use the jewel! You're totally confusing me! Should I use it or not?"

"Kara, your ice cream's getting cold!" Kyle yelled.

Kara looked over at her friends. "Be right there!"

When she looked back, the figures were gone. The fountain was calm, water gently cascading down the marble as if nothing had happened.

12

KARA FELT RELIEVED when the party finally wound down. Kyle and his friends went to Joey's to check out some new video game, and not long after that, Molly's mom arrived to pick up the girls.

Kara cleaned up quickly, then headed to the sunroom for a nice hot soak in the Jacuzzi.

The glass-walled extension had been built onto the side of the house. The air was moist and heavy with the scent of flowers, trees bearing ripening fruit, and the hot steam of the Jacuzzi.

Kara was worn out. Thank goodness her mom had left the Jacuzzi heater on. She turned on the timer for the jets. Instantly the water in the large sunken tub began to churn and bubble. This is too bizarre, Kara thought as she changed into her bathing suit in the screened-off dressing area. The cat, and then the dragonflies . . . and what exactly were those watery things? What were they trying to say to me? And why me?

Fingers of steam crept into the dressing area, covering everything in soft mist. Kara stood before the mirror to admire herself. She turned the jewel around in her hands, studying its sparkling surfaces. Whatever was going on, it had something to do with this. She examined the jewel closely. Flecks of pure diamond radiated from the delicately scalloped shape. It was exquisite.

Yet something about it looked familiar. The shape. Where had she seen such an incredible crystalline form before?

It was hypnotic, sparkling with brilliance, yet below the surface, Kara could feel tremendous power pulsing like a mighty river.

Gingerly, she felt for the magic, letting her senses reach out. Prickling energy ran up and down her arms and through her hair. Kara felt light-headed as magic surged through the very core of her being. It was like nothing she had ever felt before—strange, wild, and wonderful!

She realized she was breathing too fast as the force crested like a tidal wave. Suddenly she was terrified of losing control. She frantically willed it to stop. Electricity pulsed through her body, trailing off her fingertips like faint static.

Just imagine what would happen if she *really* let the power go! Awesome!

"Mirror, mirror, on the wall, is this the coolest jewel of them all?"

A dull spark flashed in the misted glass. Kara wiped away the steam and regarded her reflection. Something wasn't quite right. Age lines creased out from her eyes, a streak of white parted her blond hair like a lightning bolt. Her skin looked cool, alabaster like a porcelain doll—had her summer tan faded already? And her eyes . . . Kara looked closer. Shivers ran up and down her spine. They weren't human. They were the slitted eyes of an animal!

Kara blinked. And her own adorable face looked back through clouds of mist.

Oh, boy, I really need to soak!

She removed her necklace and placed it on the dressing table, then padded over to the sunken tub and eased into the hot water. *Oh, heaven!* It felt wonderful. Bubbles, bubbles, lost in the bubbles. Steam circled up and enveloped her, so warm, so soothing, so nice . . .

Kara lay back and dunked her head.

Under water, bubbles churned around her, all thoughts of magic floating away . . .

The timer shut off, abruptly bringing the water to a dead calm.

Kara resurfaced, head and toes pointing out of the still water.

A single drop emerged from the jet, swirling with colors as it rose in the water. Kara watched through half-closed eyes, totally relaxed, as fluid shapes spread around her.

The drop enlarged, swelling like a balloon. The surface colors took on shapes, oily smears on water. Slimy colors turned muddy brown and green as long, stringy hair fanned from the bubble.

Kara held up a finger. Thick slime, like pond scum, dripped into the water. Her eyes flew open. She was lying in putrid green-and-brown water. In front of her, the banshee hissed as its foul head surfaced.

13

*T*HE MONSTER EXPLODED out of the slimy water.

Kara screamed and scrambled from the sunken tub, splashing water everywhere. The ragged creature began to slosh its way—not toward Kara, but to the dressing table. The jewel! The banshee was after her magic jewel! Outside, Lyra scratched wildly at the closed glass door.

Kara ran around the tub but slipped on the wet tiles. Flailing about, she grabbed a towel hanging on the rack.

"Help—*oohhf!*"

The towel rack broke and Kara tumbled into the silk screen, falling forward and collapsing to the floor. She whirled and kicked the whole mass of screen, towels, and bathing suits at the banshee. The creature wailed, batting aside the debris. Kara got to her feet and lunged for the jewel. Behind her, the banshee fought free and lurched forward. It snatched at the mat under Kara's feet, sending her flying into a citrus tree. Sobbing, Kara watched in horror as the tree came crashing down against the dressing table in a rain of dirt, leaves, and tiny oranges. Her magic jewel careened across the tile floor toward the drain in the center of the room. It caught in the grate, sparkling like a diamond.

Outstretched ragged fingers reached for the stone.

Now or never!

Kara dove headfirst toward the jewel—and jerked to a stop.

The banshee had Kara's hair caught in its grip. Kara was wrenched upward. She reached desperately for the jewel but was yanked back again. Her hair was beginning to sizzle, burning under the banshee's acid touch. Kara screamed, inhaling the sickening smell of singed hair. She pulled away sharply. But she lost her footing and slipped again, crashing against the washstand.

Through her tears, Kara watched the creature's clawed, twisted hand reach out . . .

Suddenly the jewel rose into the air.

"KeeKee!"

"Goldie!" Kara exclaimed. Eyes red with fury, the banshee howled as it grabbed for the stone. But the jewel floated just out of its grasp.

Four more dragonflies popped into the room in bursts of light.

"Skeepooot!"

The banshee swatted at them, trying to get at the jewel.

"Here, over here! Good dragonflies!" Kara called out.

Goldie swooped toward Kara, the jewel wobbling in her tiny claws. She dropped it into Kara's outstretched hand.

Kara spun to face the banshee, holding the jewel out in front of her. "Stay back!" she screamed. She didn't know what to do. Should she use it, or not?

The banshee lumbered forward with sloppy wet steps and reached out.

Kara held the stone and concentrated on driving the creature back.

Astonishment and terror chased across the hideous face. The banshee's red eyes filled with despair, and the creature fell back, covering its face with clawed hands.

Kara threw her arms theatrically into the air and called on the power of the stone. *Make lightning smite the banshee into a million, million pieces!*

"Go away, scary thing!" she shouted wildly.

Power rushed through her like a freight train, sending circles of light swirling around her body.

The banshee cowered before the blazing magic.

Kara laughed triumphantly. Nobody was going to take her jewel. The creature began shrinking, falling in on itself, its rags spreading out across the tiled floor into a puddle of slime. Clawed fingers reached out in a desperate plea.

"You doom us all . . ."

Kara watched, amazed, as matted hair swirled around in clumps. With a final gurgle, the thing turned to green slime and vanished down the drain.

14

"AND DON'T COME back!" Kara wiped her hands together.

A strange light gleamed behind her.

She slowly turned.

The mirror's surface swirled, as if filled with mist. Cold animal eyes glinted, distant and cruel—then faded. Kara's own wide blue eyes stared back from the cool reflective glass.

A trick of the light?

Kara looked closer at the disheveled blond hair sticking out over her ears.

What?

Carefully, she touched the back of her head and felt the short, stiff ends.

She whirled around and looked over her shoulder. An entire section of her hair was gone, singed off by the banshee. It was as if a mad barber had run a lawn mower up her neck and onto the back of her head.

"My hair!" Kara burst into tears.

Lyra was carefully picking her way through the wreckage. *"Hair isn't important."*

"Maybe not to you!" Kara wailed.

The cat regarded her with deep, calm eyes.

"What am I going to do?" Tears spilled down Kara's cheeks.

"It will grow back," said Lyra.

"I can't wait that long," Kara cried, her voice trembling. "What do I tell my parents and everybody in school? I can't tell them about that thing, I can't tell them about the jewel, and I can't tell them about *you!*"

She sniffled, trying to control herself. "I've got to fix this on my own."

"How?" Lyra asked suspiciously.

"Magic," Kara answered. "And you're going to help me!"

The cat cocked her head.

Kara clutched the gemstone in one hand and put her other on the back of her head. "Stand still and help me make magic."

"All right," the cat answered, moving next to her. *"Breathe calmly, and we'll focus together."*

Kara took a deep breath.

Hair! It must, *must* grow, she thought. She closed her eyes tight and concentrated with all her might on how much she needed this to happen, right now.

Grow!

Kara pressed closer to Lyra. The gem grew warm and she thought she could feel a faint tingling on her scalp. And then her hand, clutching the cropped hair, dropped toward her shoulder. Her eyes flew open.

Yes! Her hair was definitely growing!

"*Is it working?*" Lyra asked.

"You tell me."

Puzzled, the cat looked into the mirror. Not only was Kara's hair growing, but the fur all over the cat's body was growing as well. Lustrous spotted fur now covered the bald and scarred patches.

"Look at you!" Kara said in delight.

Lyra's body was bushy with new fur. "*This is not funny.*"

"Skeehee!"

"Leeloo!"

The dragonflies somersaulted happily.

Kara pulled her hand away and twirled around, hair flying out in a golden cascade. She hugged Lyra, laughing with sheer relief.

"Oh, thank goodness!" she cried. "I'll have to get a trim, but at least I won't be going back to school looking diseased." She pulled a pink scrunchie around her hair.

Lyra examined herself in the mirror. "*I think we might have grown enough hair.*"

Kara felt her scrunchie drop lower . . . down her neck . . . past her shoulders . . . Her hair was growing faster and faster. "Stop! Stop, please!" she yelled at her stone.

Nothing stopped. The scrunchie dropped toward her waist. Lyra was beginning to look like a woolly mammoth. "I take it back," Kara cried. "Reverse the magic!"

But the scrunchie didn't stop dropping as her hair reached her feet. "What do we do?" Kara sobbed.

"This was your idea. Make it stop," Lyra said.

Kara closed her eyes and concentrated, waving the jewel all around, but the hair kept growing. "I can't."

The dragonflies darted this way and that, lifting up long golden strands.

Kara began to cry again as waves of hair piled onto the floor.

"Stop crying, we have enough water already!" Lyra looked like a walking shaggy carpet.

"I have to call Emily," Kara finally decided. "We need help and fast!"

She stepped over mountains of hair, grabbed the phone from the wall, and punched in Emily's number.

"Hello?"

"Uh, hello," Kara squeaked.

"Kara, are you all right?" Emily instantly sensed that something was wrong.

"No!"

"What happened?"

"Can you come over here, like, right now?"

"You used the jewel!" Emily accused.

"Just get over here and hurry! I'm in the sunroom out back."

"Okay, hang on, I'll call Adriane. We'll be right there." Emily hung up.

With a grunt, Kara twisted the new hair, using four scrunchies to keep it together. It was a thick cable now, bumping along on the floor behind her. The big furry cat lumbered over.

Kara couldn't help laughing. "You look like Cousin It!"

"Who?" Lyra asked.

"Pheeheee!"

"Hoohaa . . ."

"Oooohoo!"

Four dragonflies landed on Kara's arms and lap. A purple one sat on Lyra, scratching the cat's back. Lyra closed her eyes and flopped down next to Kara.

"How did you get in here, anyway?" Kara asked Lyra as she petted the mini dragon's head.

"Up there," Lyra said, opening one eye and cocking her head skyward.

Kara looked up. The sunroom skylight was open. This cat was very agile!

She brushed Lyra's long, silky fur coat. "Nice coloring, it's beautiful."

"I didn't think it would ever grow back."

"So what happened to you, I mean, your fur?"

"I was burned trying to escape," Lyra told her.

"Escape from where?"

"A place called the Shadowlands." Her fur bristled.

"What were you doing there?" Kara stroked her fur back down.

"There was a raid in my forest. Hunters took us to a powerful sorceress."

Kara's eyes widened. She suddenly flashed on what the magic water things had told her about the Dark Sorceress. Shivering, Kara snuggled closer.

"We were brought to a dungeon and locked in with other animals. The sorceress was stealing our magic. I was the only one in our group who escaped. I tried to save my sisters, but I couldn't."

"That's the saddest thing I ever heard!" Kara burst into tears again, sobbing into the cat's silken side.

"Boohoop . . ."

"Aaahhhooooh . . ."

The dragonflies were crying all over Kara and Lyra.

"Do not cry for me." Lyra gazed into Kara's eyes. *"There is enough sadness in my world."*

Kara sniffled. "Do you think they're all right, your sisters?"

"I don't know. I was chased by the manticore and hardly remember falling through the portal into this world. Adriane found me, and Emily helped me to heal. When I discovered the other animals had been burned by the Black Fire, too, I realized I could not fight the sorceress and her dark creatures myself."

"Like the manticore and these banshees?"

"Oooo!"

"Skweek!"

Kara stroked the agitated dragonflies.

"*The banshees have also suffered at the hands of this sorceress. She would destroy our whole world to get what she wants.*"

"What does she want?"

"*Magic.*"

"I thought I wanted magic." Kara buried her head in the cat's still-growing fur. "I'm just stupid! Look what I did!"

"*Things are not always what they seem.*"

"They're not?"

"*You must look beyond what your eyes see, and what your fingers touch. Magic always starts from the heart, Kara.*"

"Do you think I'll ever learn how to make good magic?" Kara asked shyly.

"*Yes, I do. A true heart makes true magic.*"

Kara looked into Lyra's warm green eyes and smiled.

There was a knock on the glass door. "Kara, are you in there? It's Emily."

"Yes! We're in here!" Kara jumped up, sending the dragonflies flapping away. Deep piles of hair tangled around her ankles as she ran to open the door.

Emily and Adriane walked into the sunroom, mouths agape.

"FoooF!" Ozzie foofed, disappearing into the golden froth.

"What happened in here?" Adriane asked, surveying the hair-filled disaster area.

"We told you not to use that jewel!" Emily sounded really mad.

Kara burst into tears. "I *had* to," she sobbed, and she told them all about Lyra, the dragonflies, the barbecue, the water thingies, the banshee attack, and—worst of all—her hair.

"Talk about a bad hair day," Adriane said, looking with interest at the blue dragonfly that had landed on her shoulder.

"You have to help me!" Kara wailed. "My parents will be home soon!"

Waves of blond hair lapped halfway up the glass walls. Four dragonflies hovered and chattered at one another, examining a moving lump of hair.

"Go away, you pests!" Ozzie called, his voice muffled.

"They helped me," Kara explained. "That's Barney, Goldie, Blaze, and Fred."

"You *named* them?" Adriane said, half smiling as she scratched blue Fred's head.

"Well, yeah . . . So?"

"Keekee!" A red one hovered in front of Kara and spit out a burst of color. "Oh, and that's Fiona."

"OooO!" Fiona dashed off.

"Look at *you!*" Emily picked her way over to the shaggy cat. Lyra rubbed against Emily's side. "Incredible! I tried to make her fur grow back and couldn't do it . . ."

For a moment she faltered, but then she smiled. "This is wonderful, Kara!" Emily gave Lyra a hug.

"Kara, what did you do?" Adriane asked. "You just ordered it to grow?"

"Yes," she replied, shame-faced.

"Well, let's just cut it," Adriane proposed.

Emily shook her head. "We need to reverse this grow-spell, like, right now." She fished around in the hair for Ozzie and hoisted him up. "Suggestions?"

"*Ptui!* I think Adriane's jewel would be the most effective, since she and Storm have been practicing together." He turned to Adriane. "Can you call Storm?"

Adriane closed her eyes. Instantly, a ribbon of mist snaked through the door and Stormbringer materialized at her side.

"Looks like a hairy situation." The wolf's golden eyes sparkled.

Sproing! Two scrunchies snapped at once and blond hair spilled out, billowing around the room. Kara looked down in horror.

"Okay, Rapunzel, let's do it," Adriane said. "Picture your hair the way you want it.

The three girls stood together with Lyra, Storm, and Ozzie. The dragonflies swooped and danced all around them. Kara clutched her jewel and imagined her hair beautiful again, the most beautiful hair ever!

"Hair today, gone tomorrow," Adriane chuckled. Her striped golden stone brightened as she held up her wrist.

Kara's jewel blazed to life with bright light. "It's working!"

Suddenly more dragonflies popped into the room, filling it with color and motion. They swooped, picking up strands of hair, weaving it around the girls and their magic.

Kara concentrated super hard, feeling the power rush from her toes to her fingertips. The dragonflies themselves glimmered, their bright colors blending with the glow from the gems until the light was so intense that all three girls had to shut their eyes.

There was a burst of brilliance. Then the glow faded.

They all opened their eyes.

Kara just gaped. Festoons of hair were strung from the window and from the light fixtures, hooked over the skylight, and tangled on the trees.

And the hair wasn't blond—wasn't *just* blond—anymore. It was streaked with every color of the rainbow. Green, red, blue, purple, aqua, and pink glistened along the strands.

"Well, it seems to have stopped growing," Adriane announced.

"What do we do now?" Kara sputtered. "You can't leave me like this!"

"You're right," Adriane agreed. She opened a drawer and held up a pair of scissors. "Ready?"

Kara was speechless. She turned away and closed her eyes. "Not too short, okay?"

As Emily grabbed a big handful of brightly colored hair, Adriane started cutting. The dragonflies snatched up wads of loose hair, weaving and braiding in graceful motions, then flying out through the skylight, trailing glittering rainbow strands behind them.

"What do you think?" Emily finally asked, trimming the last bits of hair out of Kara's eyes.

Kara cautiously faced the mirror. Her hair fell just past her shoulders, like before, but it was still streaked with every color imaginable—blue, red, green, yellow, purple . . ."Oh, man . . ." she breathed.

"It's unique," Adriane said, appraising Kara's new do. "Definitely you."

"I have rainbow hair!" Kara exclaimed, horrified.

"You're welcome," Adriane said.

"What am I going to tell everyone?" Kara wailed. "You have to fix it!"

"Kara, we can't keep messing around with magic until we know what we're doing," Emily said. "I think we're lucky we did what we did."

The dragonflies were dragging the last unattached scraps of multicolored hair up through the skylight.

"Just tell everyone you got some new highlights," Adriane suggested.

"From where!" Kara screamed. "The circus?"

"You'll think of something," Emily said. "But no more magic! Okay?"

"Yeah, okay," Kara said glumly. Keeping a magic jewel secret was one thing, rainbow hair was something else.

She watched as Adriane, Ozzie, Emily, and Storm left the sunroom. She turned to see Lyra gazing at her. Her fur was perfectly restored; thick and gorgeous and just the right length.

"Well, at least one of us got it right," Kara said.

"Thank you."

"For what?"

"For helping me."

"I didn't do anything except make a total mess."

The cat licked her shoulder and walked out the door, lustrous fur shining in the moonlight.

Kara sighed. She had wanted magic and she sure had gotten it. At least it wasn't a complete disaster. She had helped Lyra. Kara had to smile. Somehow that seemed to make everything better.

15

*K*ARA CAREFULLY CHECKED herself in her locker
mirror. Her hair was tucked neatly under a pink
beret. Cute, she thought. Too bad I'll have to wear it till
like . . . *forever!*

"Kara, come *on*, we're late!"

Kara turned to see Molly charging toward her.
"Assembly, remember? Everyone's there already."

"Oh, yeah, I forgot. Let's go, Mol." Kara adjusted
her blue blazer, linked arms with Molly, and headed
down the hall. She could get lost in the crowd for a
while. Perfect.

The auditorium was filled to capacity. Kids were
yelling, tossing balls of paper, hip-hopping in their seats,
and creating general assembly mayhem.

"Kara, Molly, over here!" Tiffany waved from where she and Heather had saved two seats. "Hey, cute hat," she said, reaching out to touch the beret as Kara slid in next to her.

Kara jerked away.

"What's up with you?" Tiffany laughed.

"Oh, it's . . . new," Kara said quickly.

"This sure beats homeroom, huh?" Heather commented, leaning across Tiffany.

"Look at Marsha Luff's dress, do you believe it?" Tiffany murmured.

"What about Lori Eller's hair!" Heather squealed.

At least it's only two colors. Kara sat back, eyes darting back and forth.

Feedback squawked from the stage.

"Okay then," Principal Edwards said, poking the microphone. "Settle down, everyone."

The general mayhem settled to a quieter general mayhem, a few giggles and laughs cutting through.

"On behalf of the school board, I'd like to welcome you all to a new year at Stonehill Middle School. We have our first pep rally tomorrow afternoon, the Harvest Ball dance next month, and the best football team ever, right, Coach?"

Coach Berman raised his arms in triumph as a bunch of boys cheered from the back of the auditorium.

"Stonehill rocks!" someone yelled.

Kara started to relax as Mr. Edwards continued his

welcome-to-school speech. *Okay, this is working. No one will notice me—*

A *pop* sounded under her seat.

Heather and Tiffany looked at her.

"S'cuse me," Kara said, patting her tummy.

"Pook?"

"Go away!" Kara whispered, dropping her books on the floor.

"Splaaa . . ." Fiona disappeared in a burst of red.

"Along with sports, we also pride ourselves on academics and community service," Mr. Edwards was saying.

Pop! Pop! Pop!

Kara look around. *Oh, no, those little—where were they?*

"We have some terrific school projects planned for this year," the principal continued, "and some of our students are getting involved in community projects, building leadership and responsibility, working to help our town, demonstrating qualities we can all be proud of."

"Woohoot!" Blaze hung down from the front of Kara's beret. She shoved him inside and adjusted the hat, smiling as Tiffany gave her a quick look.

"The mayor has commissioned a group of students to work on something we can all share in, the Ravenswood Wildlife Preservation Society." Principal Edwards beamed.

What?

"Keekee, play!" Barney pulled at Kara's finger. He was sitting in her lap.

She squashed the purple pest into the pocket of her jacket.

The principal was looking around the auditorium for someone.

Oh, no! Kara shrank down in her seat. Do *not* go there!

"And the town council has appointed Kara Davies president of the Ravenswood project."

Kara slid farther down into her seat as whistles and laughter went up from the crowd.

"Kara, come up." The principal beckoned. "I know this is unscheduled, but we're so proud of the example you're setting for the entire student body. Come on up and tell us about the great work you'll be doing."

"No, thank you," Kara squeaked.

"Kara!" Tiffany laughed. "Get up there!"

"I, like, *so* do not want to go up there!"

But her friends were already pushing her from her seat. This has got to be a bad dream, no, a horrible nightmare, she thought, walking onto the stage.

"Thank you, Mr. Edwards."

"Weekoook."

Kara pulled down hard on her hat.

"So tell us, Kara, are you excited to be president of the new organization?"

"Huh? Oh, yeah, it's good to help animals." What a lame-o, she thought, mortified.

"Uh-huh . . ." The principal was looking at her expectantly.

"We hope to open the preserve again soon and teach people about conservation and protecting wildlife, and we have our own web—'Skooo'—too." Kara slapped her pocket.

Startled, Mr. Edwards glanced at her. "Excellent. Let's have a hand for a fine example of one of Stonehill's most promising young people."

Kara sent her best smile into the audience.

"Kookoo!"

Kara slapped her head—and felt hair. Out of the corner of her eye something moved. Kara watched in horror as her pink beret slowly inched across the stage floor. She shot out her foot and pinned it down.

"KaAsplaaP!"

The auditorium fell silent. Heather, Molly, and Tiffany sat with mouths agape.

Uh-oh.

Kara's hair unfurled like a bright neon rainbow flag.

She felt the hot flush run from her shoulders to her face as the auditorium suddenly erupted in hoots, jeers, and hollers.

Kara stood in the middle of the stage, alone, her world falling apart.

"Ms. Davies!" the principal said in shock. "What is the meaning of this outrageous display?"

Kara felt two inches tall. She was being reprimanded by the principal in front of the entire school. This was it, her life was over. She'd be the laughingstock of the school forever.

"It's symbolic!" someone yelled from the middle of the auditorium.

All eyes turned to the girl who had stood up. It was Emily.

Kara froze. This was much worse than any monster she had faced.

"Beg pardon, young lady?" the principal asked Emily.

"Kara is symbolizing the true meaning of the Ravenswood Wildlife Preservation Society, a rainbow coalition of all species working together. We live in one world, so everyone should work together to save the animals and our planet."

The principal looked at Kara expectantly.

She nodded quickly, smile frozen in place.

"Ms. Davies!"

Kara flinched.

"Fabulous!" He beamed. "Truly inspired! What a wonderful symbolic message to the world!"

Kara took over, instincts kicking in. "Thank you, thank you. Let's all work together to make our world a better place." She raised her fist in the air. "Animals are people, too!"

The crowd went crazy, cheering and clapping, as Kara left the stage, the envy of everyone.

Mr. Edwards was scratching his head but smiling. "Thank you, and welcome to another school year."

With assembly over, everyone bolted for the doors. Molly, Tiffany, and Heather came running through the crowd as kids pressed in to look at Kara's amazing hair.

"Oh, Kara, it's gorgeous!"

"Kara, that is the coolest thing ever!"

Emily and Adriane stood in the hall, waiting to one side as the students spilled out. Kara was all smiles, grinning ear to ear.

Pushing past the crowd, Kara crossed over to Emily. "That was incredible, what you just did," she whispered.

Emily smiled. "That's what friends are for."

16

$\mathcal{A}$T LUNCHTIME, KARA walked through the cafeteria to cheers and waves.

"Kara, over here!" Tiffany, Heather, and Molly had saved prime spots under the shade of a sprawling oak. Kyle, Marcus, and Joey sat nearby with trays overflowing with spaghetti.

A quick scan of the area revealed no sign of those pesky dragonflies and no wild animal sightings. Kara crossed the lawn to join her friends, her rainbow-bright hair flowing in the wind.

"Kara, you are something else!" Marcus said.

"Yeah, no wonder the place was a mess last night," Kyle snickered. "Mom and Dad yelled at me, but I told them it was all your fault."

"Thanks, you're a pal," Kara said, sitting down.

"Why didn't you say something?" Tiffany asked.

"Spill it, girl, how'd you do it?" Heather studied Kara's hair.

"There must be a hundred colors!" Molly exclaimed.

Kara noticed Emily and Adriane coming out of the cafeteria, balancing trays and surveying the crowded tables.

"Well, I had some help." Kara waved. "Emily! Over here!" She ignored the look Heather and Tiffany gave each other.

Emily tapped Adriane and nodded in Kara's direction. They walked over, Adriane scowling behind Emily.

Heather frowned. "Do we have to sit with them?"

Kara ignored her.

"No wonder you wanted to end the barbecue early," Tiffany said. "You were planning this all along!"

"Believe me, no one was as surprised as I was," Kara replied.

Molly slid over to make room for Emily. "I just love what you did with Kara's hair. It's so original. Could you do mine, too?"

"It wouldn't be original then, would it?" Adriane smirked as she took a seat beside Emily.

Once again, Kara found herself in the middle: Emily and Adriane on one side, Tiffany, Heather, and Molly on the other. Well, this is interesting, she mused. No nuclear explosions . . . yet.

"Oh, I don't care." Molly smiled. "I think it's so rad!"

"Actually, it was Adriane who did my hair." Kara glanced at Adriane and held out a hank of multicolored hair for everybody to admire again.

Tiffany and Heather looked shocked. "What?"

"Who'd a thunk under all that black is a fashion designer!" Kyle called out.

"I'm not big on fashion," Adriane said quietly.

"That's for sure," Heather said out of the corner of her mouth.

Adriane glowered, putting her hands on the table. Her loose lanyard bracelet slid down her wrist to reveal her tigereye jewel. It flashed with bright gold light.

Heather's eyes widened. "How did it do that?"

"They react to light," Emily said quickly. Trying to distract attention from Adriane's jewel, she showed them her own rainbow jewel in its simple woven bracelet.

"You have one, too?" Molly gazed in awe at Emily's bright stone. "Where can we get them?"

"These jewels are totally unique," Kara explained, twirling her own on her silver necklace. "You can't get one."

"*They* have one!" Tiffany huffed.

"All part of our plan to get attention for the preserve," Emily told them.

"Can we come and check it out, too?" Molly asked excitedly.

"And get our own light-up jewels?" Heather echoed.

"*No!* Uh . . . I mean—" Adriane flushed.

"Of course you can visit the preserve," Emily said. "But we have a lot of work to do there first."

As Kara listened, she couldn't help but be struck by the realization that her friends—Heather, Tiffany, and Molly—only days ago were totally making fun of the preserve. And now, they were, like, all over it, all because they wanted "light-up" jewels. That is so shallow, Kara thought. And she knew she'd been exactly the same way. Or maybe she still *was* exactly the same way.

"The whole point is helping animals," Emily said.

"Just wait till you hear about the big fund-raising party," Kara told them. "We're going to have music, just like Live Aid!"

"Excellent! We're in on that!" Heather's eyes lit up.

Marcus glanced over. "Yeah, like who?"

"Well . . . Linny Lewis or Sampleton Malls, maybe."

"Choke! That is so lame!" Joey sauntered over, brushing back a lock of dark hair from his face. "What about Toad Force?"

"Or Smash Fish," Adriane put in.

Joey looked at her in surprise. "Yeah, all right!"

Kara almost laughed. Had Adriane actually blushed? She looked again, but Adriane was studying her tray as the boys moved off, heading back inside.

"Hey, rainbow girl!" Kyle called over his shoulder. "Press is here!"

Two eighth graders approached, carrying cameras and notepads. "Can we get a picture for the Stonehill Journal?"

"Cool. Sure." Kara stood and fluffed her hair, fanning out the bright colors.

"Right. Outstanding hair," the older girl said, snapping a picture.

"Thank you, it's symbolic."

The girl with the camera stepped forward. "How about a group picture?"

"Come on girls, photo op," Kara said, pulling Emily and Adriane over to her.

Side by side they stood, three together, Kara in the middle, rainbow hair flaring behind her. She put an arm around each girl and actually felt a connection, the bond of Ravenswood—and magic.

TO: Daddy1@townhall.hill.net
RE: RWPS update
Hey Daddy,
Guess who? It's me! We're getting our picture in the paper, Emily, Adriane and me for the Ravenswood Wildlife Preservation Society, isn't that cool? I know you will be so proud. Oh, and don't freak out when you see my hair, it's symbolic. I'll explain later. That's where we are on the RWPS for now.

Kara sat in study hall, laptop open in front of her. But

her eyes kept wandering toward the window in search of unidentified flying animals. Ravenswood was on the map now whether she liked it or not. Everyone knew about it. But wasn't that the point? Wasn't that why the town council had allowed the girls to keep the preserve open and get the website up?

Of course it was, and she was doing a fantastic job. Even Emily and Adriane had to admit it. So why couldn't they just fit in with her group? Why did she have to do this juggling act? No matter what she did, it seemed someone got hurt. And that made her feel . . . awful.

Emily was sweet and pretty sharp. Kara was growing to like her more and more, and after that amazing save this morning, she owed Emily big time. And Kara got the feeling Emily wouldn't hold it over her, wouldn't expect anything in return except to be treated with respect and an open mind. Is that what made a real friend?

But Adriane—Kara and that girl would never get along, end of story. They were just too different, they had nothing in common. Kara twisted the sparkling jewel in her hand. Except this: magic.

Kara sighed and went back to her e-mail. Funny—the words looked wrong. She rubbed her eyes. The letters seemed weird. She looked closer. Words were stretching and starting to move around the screen. How bizarre!

Suddenly she felt her stone pulsing like a heartbeat.

The words on the screen were stretching, shifting around like pieces of a puzzle.

I

The letter turned red and started to melt down the screen.

know

Words from her e-mail were fading . . .

who

. . . leaving only a few that turned red.

you

The last words remained . . .

are

. . . dripping like blood.

I know who you are.

Fear crept up her spine. She shivered, quickly hitting keys to try to clear the screen. Nothing worked. Who was sending this?

Blood-red letters melted down the screen around two hard, cold eyes that stared at Kara. They were magnetic and vicious—half-human, half-animal. Kara froze. It was the same evil face she'd seen in the mirror.

The animal-woman pointed a finger and the laptop screen seemed to stretch, bulging outward. Kara's stomach knotted in fear as a sharp silver claw pushed through the screen, reaching for her.

She gasped and slammed the laptop closed.

I know who you are.

17

"*T*HAT'S *IT*!" KARA stormed into the Ravenswood Manor library. Emily and Adriane were sitting before the computer screen, scrolling through information. Balthazar, Ozzie, and Ronif peered over the girls' shoulders.

"Something is in my computer," Kara announced angrily.

They all turned to stare at Kara.

"Your computer?" Emily echoed.

Kara dumped her backpack on a table, pulled out her pink laptop, and handed it to Emily. "Look!" she said. "Please."

Emily flipped open the laptop and turned it on.

Adriane came around to watch. Kara backed away, nervously twirling a strand of purple hair in her fingers.

"Oh, no!" Adriane exclaimed in horror.

Kara jumped back. "Be careful! I told you!"

Adriane turned the computer toward Kara. The screen displayed her desktop with the new Linny Lewis wallpaper she had made.

"Linny Lewis is after you?" Adriane laughed.

"*No!* Lemme see that!" Kara marched over to look.

To her relief, the screen was perfectly normal. "Something weird is going on around here," she said.

"You mean weirder than normal?" Adriane asked.

"Yeeaaah . . ." Kara said, looking into the faces of a talking ferret, two quiffles, and a pegasus.

"Maybe your computer has a virus," Emily ventured.

Kara shook her head. "Someone left a message."

"What message?"

"It said, 'I know who you are.'" Kara shivered. "How creepy is that?"

"Maybe it read the Stonehill Journal," Adriane cracked.

"Oh, very funny! And if she did, she'd know who *you* are, too! But it's all happening to me!"

"She?" Balthazar asked.

"I think so. She had these weird eyes." Kara twisted her gem in her hand.

"That jewel," Adriane said. "It's been nothing but trouble!"

Kara glared at her.

"Kara," Emily said, "ever since you found it, these creatures have been after you, right?"

Kara swallowed. "Um . . . sorta . . . maybe."

"Maybe what?" Adriane asked.

"The night *before* I found this jewel, one of those banshees was in my room. It took my pink sweater. Why did it do that?"

Emily turned back to the computer screen. "We've found some files that Mr. Gardener left." She clicked on a book-shaped icon. A heading in an old-fashioned scroll spread across the top of the page. "Creatures of Magic." Below was a list of names, each accompanied by a picture.

Emily scrolled down. Some of the creatures they recognized: jeerans, pegasi . . .

"There's quiffles!" Ronif exclaimed.

The creatures became darker, more bizarre, some hideously ugly and monstrous.

"Eww, creep me out!" Kara made a face.

"Any of these look familiar?" Emily asked.

"No."

"There's a manticore," Ozzie pointed out. The terrifying winged demon looked out from the screen. Even though it was only a picture, its razor teeth and blood-red eyes sent chills up and down Kara's spine as she recalled facing the real thing only weeks before.

"Wait, open that one," she instructed.

Emily clicked on the thumbnail and the screen filled

with an image of the ragged creature Kara recognized from the glade and the sunroom.

"That's *it*," Kara said, backing away. "Only it doesn't have that green stuff."

"You mean Black Fire," Balthazar nodded.

"The ones we saw looked badly poisoned," Ronif confirmed.

"Banshees," Emily read. "Creatures of fairy that have been cursed. They have long, streaming hair and ragged clothes. Eyes are fiery red from constant weeping. Banshees cry because they foretell darkness and pain."

"Like messengers of bad news?" Adriane asked.

"They were monsters, not messengers," Kara said.

"There are a lot of poor creatures on Aldenmor that wander the Shadowlands," Balthazar said. "Hideous and twisted by dark magic."

"What's the Shadowlands?" Emily asked.

"A place on Aldenmor. It used to be beautiful forests and meadows until the witch destroyed it."

"It's where Black Fire comes from," Kara informed them.

They all looked at Kara.

"Lyra told me. She was there. She was captured by hunters and brought to this castle where this . . . person was torturing animals."

"That's terrible!" Emily cried, outraged.

"Lyra escaped, but her sisters didn't." Kara felt the cat's sadness, connected to it somehow.

"We know of this Dark Sorceress," Balthazar shuddered.

"A terrible witch who hunts animals," Ronif added.

"Lyra said she's stealing magic from the animals," Kara continued.

"Trying to force animals to make magic," Ozzie grimaced. "It's a complete perversion of the magic. Horrible!"

"But we know *our* magic is stronger with our animal friends," Emily reasoned.

"And the legends that say humans and animals once worked together to make strong magic," Balthazar agreed.

"Well, now the animals have defenders to protect them!" Adriane punched her fist into her palm for emphasis.

"That's right!" Ozzie sprang to his feet. "Let's go!"

"Ozzie." Emily caught his tale and pulled the agitated ferret back. "We don't know what we're up against yet."

"But I'm not an animal," Kara argued. "Why is this sorceress after me? And she can't have my jewel!"

"Why would she want your jewel and not ours?" Adriane asked.

"Cause mine's better," Kara quipped, then added, "I don't know, but she's not getting it and neither are those banshees."

Adriane pointed back to the computer monitor. "According to this, 'Banshees foretell dark magic and the fate of those who are touched by evil.'"

"How do they do that?" Emily asked.

Adriane read on. "They wash an article of clothing of the one who is tainted."

Kara felt the blood rush from her face. "It was washing my sweater. What am I going to do? I'm tainted!" she wailed. "Do I smell bad?"

"Kara, don't you think there's something odd about your jewel?" Emily asked.

"What do you mean?"

"What did it look like when you first found it?" Adriane asked Kara.

"Just like this." Kara held out the dazzling gem.

"Ours changed as we used them, as if they became tuned to us."

"That would make sense," Ozzie added. "Magic jewels are tuned to a specific person. Only they can use it."

"Well, mine got here all powerful and ready to go. So what?" Kara clutched the stone close. "Just takes some time to learn to work it right." But she knew she had none of the control Emily and Adriane had over their magic.

"Kara, maybe that jewel is not for you," Emily said slowly.

"How do you know when a jewel is really for you?" Kara held up the magic stone. Bright facets cast sparkles across her face.

"You just know, Kara," Adriane replied. "It's like they reflect a part of who we are."

"Well, those banshees aren't after *your* jewel, they're after . . . mine." Kara realized what she was saying. Her jewel was different. But how? What part of her did it reflect? Did the banshees know *she* would be the one to find this jewel? Was she tainted with dark magic?

"If this sorceress is hunting animals, she may want the jewel to trap an animal," Balthazar suggested.

"Oh, no!" Kara's mouth opened in horror. "Do you think she's after Lyra?"

"Kara, this isn't just your problem," Emily said.

"We're in this together," Adriane agreed.

"That's right, we all are," Ozzie said, waving a paw to include the other animals.

"So what do we do?" Kara asked.

"Whoever is after that jewel will come back for it." Adriane looked at the others. "We'll just have to be ready to deal with it."

"So I'm supposed to wait around like a sitting quiffle?" Kara complained. "No offense," she said to Ronif.

"Those water creatures told you the jewel is a trap, right?" Emily said.

"Yeah . . . but they were confusing me and I sat on one."

"We think they were Fairimentals, like the ones that came to us made of earth and twigs," Emily explained.

"Kara," Ozzie said. "The Fairimentals sent me to find three human mages, a healer, a warrior, and a blazing star."

"So?"

"So . . . we don't know what a blazing star is . . ."

"What's your point?"

"Maybe you're not the one . . ." Ozzie said cautiously. "The blazing star."

Kara was speechless. How could she *not* be the blazing star? She found the most fabulous jewel! Had she only found it by accident?

"But Ozzie," Emily said. "Kara makes magic happen stronger when she's around us."

"So do we," Ronif pointed out.

"What, so now I'm like a magical animal?" Kara scoffed.

Ozzie tapped his chin thoughtfully. "Kara obviously conducts magic, like the animals do, so maybe the jewel is a test."

"A test? Why are they testing me and not Emily and Adriane?"

"Maybe they're being tested in different ways. But this time the Fairimentals came to you. We don't know what a blazing star is. But three mages are needed to help Aldenmor and the animals."

"I want this to be mine so bad!" Kara admitted, holding the crystal tightly. But even if it only attracts bad magic?

"I'll ask Storm to watch out for you," Adriane offered.

"All the animals are on the look-out for anything unusual," Ozzie put in.

"So, are we all agreed?" Emily asked.

Adriane and the animals nodded.

"All right," Emily said. "In the meantime, we continue to sort out this website information and separate what we want to hide."

"Mr. Gardener left us a lot of stuff here," Adriane said.

"Yeah, and look what happened to him," Kara moaned.

"We don't know what's happened to him," Adriane pointed out.

"Exactly!" Kara grabbed her backpack and laptop. "Okay, I can't believe I'm saying this, but I'm going home to do homework. Maybe it will take my mind off this crazy stuff."

"Okay, but no more magic," Emily cautioned.

"Yes, Mother."

"Anything happens, you call us, right?" Adriane prompted.

"Yes, Father."

Adriane narrowed her eyes, then smiled. Kara smiled back, and suddenly everyone broke out laughing. Kara tried to hold the good feelings close, a shield to push back her fears. But inside she could not help but think about what the banshees foretold: dark things were coming. How were they supposed to fight a sorceress destroying an entire world when they barely understood their magic?

Ozzie had been sent from Aldenmor to find three mages. The healer, which Emily had proven herself to be, the warrior, who could only be Adriane, and a blazing star. She was undoubtedly a star: smart, cute, the center of attention, impeccably groomed—but was that enough? She couldn't ignore the awful feeling that something wasn't right. That she might not be good enough. But one thing had become crystal clear. Kara wanted this more than anything in her whole life. And she always got what she wanted.

18

THE REST OF the week went by in double Kara time as she dove into a whirlwind of school and social activities. It was almost as if things were . . . normal. Well, as normal as they can be when your hair is a hundred different colors and then some.

On Saturday morning, Mrs. Davies dropped Kara at the Stonehill Galleria Mall. The enormous glass-and-chrome complex might have been daunting to some, but not to Kara. Huge skylights capped the ceilings and mirrored hallways ran past stores, all leading to the coin-scattered fountains and immense food court in the central atrium. She cruised the main floor past Eddie Bauer, Foot Locker, Hot Topic, Sharper Image, and The

Gap. Chic fall fashions decked the window displays and SALE signs beckoned. Maybe later, she thought, when her hair wouldn't clash with everything she tried on.

The food court was packed; some cooking show was giving product demonstrations and handing out free samples. Heading up the escalator, she spotted Heather and Molly going into Banana Republic. "Hey, homegirls! See anything good?" she called out cheerfully.

Molly waved back. "Just starting here. Then looping the place."

"Where's Tiff?"

Heather pointed to Tiffany, who held up a black three-quarter sleeve wrap top. Kara gave her a thumbs-up. Thrilled, Tiffany dove back into the racks.

"Meet us at the food court, K!" Heather called.

"Okay!" Kara rounded the second-floor escalator and headed up to the third floor.

The Clip Joint was in the corner, full of mirrors, funky chemical smells, and cool gray light from skylights that reflected an overcast sky. Lightning flashed, buried in the clouds. A few raindrops spattered on the glass, but inside it was warm and dry. Customers draped in gray chatted and leafed through magazines as hairdressers in black T-shirts and pants combed and cut and colored and coiffed.

Kara walked up to the receptionist, a girl with spiky black hair. "Hi, I'm Kara Davies. I have an appointment."

"Great hair! How did you get those highlights so bright?"

"It was a mixture of things," Kara replied. "But I want my original color back."

"Angela," the girl yelled to the back of the shop, "rainbow girl is here!"

A young woman with short blond hair came bustling across the room. "Come on back." Angela led Kara to a sink and sat her down. "Just relax, we'll get this water nice and warm," she said, wrapping a towel around Kara's neck and turning on the water. "I'll be just a minute."

"Okay." Kara sat with her back to the sink, looking at her rainbow reflections in the mirrors. Her hair was pretty amazing, she had to admit. Maybe I should keep it, she thought with a giggle.

A drop of water hit her in the face.

Kara glanced over into the sink.

"Web runner," whispered a familiar high-pitched voice. A tiny liquid figure swirled out of the steamy water. Another Fairimental. It was only inches high, its voice almost lost in the noise of the shop. Kara looked around. No one was paying any attention.

"Are you a Fairimental?" Kara whispered.

"I am water . . ."

Kara could see that the figure was struggling to hold its shape. She felt the great exertion and powerful magic it took for the Fairimental to come here.

"Look, what do I do with this jewel?" Kara asked quickly. "I can't make it work right."

"Some things are yours only for a short time," the watermental gurgled.

Oh no! Had Ozzie been right after all? Maybe she wasn't the blazing star.

"Beware, the Dark Sorceress is coming . . ."

Kara shuddered. "Is Lyra in danger?"

"She wants *you* . . ."

"I don't understand." Kara bit her lip. "What does she want from me?"

"Your magic."

Kara quickly glanced around the shop. Everything seemed normal. No one had noticed her talking to the sink. When she looked back, the Fairimental was gone. *My magic?* The water thingy said *my* magic. Her jewel hung around her neck, pulsing with diamond light.

"You sure you want to bleach this color out?" Angela said, returning to the sink.

Kara covered the jewel with her hands. "Yes."

Angela adjusted the chair, leaning Kara back over the shiny black sink.

"Never seen anything like it," Angela admitted, lathering up the hair. Kara forced herself to relax as Angela rinsed out the shampoo and worked in the conditioner. "We need this to set for a few minutes," she told Kara. "Back in a sec."

Kara moved her neck into a more comfortable position and felt her jewel warm in her hand. *My* magic. Through half-closed eyes, she gazed at the mirror across from her.

Images of the shop flickered on the glass, dim and unreal in the cool, stark light. The glass began to shiver as ripples spread and the surface seemed to fall away. A gossamer spider's web of lines interlaced and stretched back, reaching to infinity. Cool. Must be reflecting from the toy store across the hall, she thought. A small light moved along the grid, arcing its way toward Kara.

She stared as the spot of light took form, expanding into an image: a magnificent white horse with a long, flowing mane and tail, streaking like a comet across the web. Something flashed. A crystalline horn sparkled on the horse's forehead—just like the jewel she grasped so tightly in her hand. A unicorn! The majestic creature was something out of a dream—her dream.

Swish, swish . . .

Kara felt cold air rush over her.

"I'm sorry, but you can't come in here." The receptionist was trying to keep a ragged old lady from shuffling into the salon. The tattered thing was hunched over, face hidden under a long shawl.

Swish, swish . . .

Kara jerked up. "Oh, no!" This can't be happening! Not here!

"Please, you have to leave immediately," the receptionist said to the hunched creature. Outside the doors, Kara saw *another* banshee shambling toward the salon.

She jumped to her feet. "Storm!" she hissed. "Where are you?"

She frantically searched the salon. Where was that stupid wolf when she really needed her!

"Are you all right?" It took a second for Kara to realize the voice in her head was Lyra's.

"Lyra! They're *here*! In the mall! Where are you?" she whispered urgently.

"Nearby."

Kara moved to the front window, looking for the cat. "You can't come in here. People will freak out!"

SPLAT!

A third banshee smashed into the window. Its hideous face pressed to the glass, eyes red from weeping, empty dark openings where its nose and mouth should have been.

Kara leaped back. What do I do? I have to do something!

Her jewel raged like fire against her chest.

Darting past the trio of banshees, Kara ran out of the salon and skidded into the hallway of the mall. In the mirrored wall, her hair was wild, glued together with gobs of drying conditioner and sticking out in all directions. Something moved inside the mirror. The unicorn rose up on his hind legs, shook his mane, and leaped away. Kara ran after him, the banshees shuffling behind.

Kara rushed toward the open circle of the mall's center hub. Looking over the railing of the atrium from three stories up, she saw the food court spread out below, full of people.

Swish, swish . . .

Swish, swish . . .

Kara turned. Five banshees were closing in from both sides of the hub. She backed into the railing, trapped.

Something darted through the crowd below. An animal, big and spotted like a leopard. Lyra!

"I'm up here!" Kara screamed out to the cat.

"Hey, Kara!" someone called.

Kara looked down to see Molly, Tiffany, Heather, Joey, and Marcus at one of the tables.

"Hair looks much better!" Joey called out. They all laughed.

The big cat was headed right down the center of the food court. No, Lyra! You can't be here!

A wail made Kara turn. A banshee reached for her. Kara screamed, kicking it away.

A terrifying roar split the air. Lyra leaped up on a table, scattering food and drinks. She leaped to another, trying to reach the escalators. Pandemonium erupted as people ran screaming, trying to get out of the way of the ferocious beast.

"Help!"

"A leopard loose in the mall!"

"Call security!"

"Over here!" Kara yelled, waving to Lyra.

Thunder rocked across the atrium as lightning lit the skylights overhead.

Kara whirled—right into the face of another gruesome, grasping banshee. Burning claws sank into Kara's arm.

The jewel flashed searing bright, instantly bathing Kara's arm in white light. She screamed and tried to twist away, but another banshee was at her back, filling the air with a foul, rancid sewer stink. Kara choked and tried to cover her face. A green hand was clawing at her necklace, trying to rip the silver chain from her neck.

Kara struggled to pull away and grabbed the railing. Below, police officers were entering the food court, walkie-talkies in hand as they rushed through the crowd. The view vanished as Kara lost her footing and went down, slamming into the hard floor. Her breath was knocked from her chest; she couldn't scream. Banshees clawed at her hair, her clothes, her flesh.

With a roar, Lyra crashed into the banshees, knocking them off Kara. The big cat stood crouched, teeth bared, growling dangerously at the creatures.

Kara stumbled to her feet. "Help! Help!"

"Up there!" someone yelled.

"The leopard!"

"It's got Kara!" Molly yelled.

"Oh, Kara!" Tiffany cried in panic.

Police rushed up the escalators. "Don't make any sudden moves!" they ordered.

Kara turned back. Lyra growled ferociously at the banshees, trying to keep them away. The officers thought the cat was attacking *her*!

"We have to get out of here!" she told Lyra urgently.

Lyra hissed. *"Go while I hold them off."*

The cat swiped at the banshees with a massive paw and they stumbled back.

Kara dashed around the circle all the way to the other side of the atrium. Security guards were trying to contain the crowds of curious shoppers below. The police moved cautiously toward the big cat, guns drawn.

"No!" Kara screamed. "Don't hurt her!"

Slowly fanning out, officers closed around the cat, trapping her against the balcony railing. Lyra snarled. She was surrounded.

"Kara!"

"Lyra!"

The cat crouched low and snarled. With a roar, she leaped.

The police scattered. One was too slow. Lyra's huge paws clipped his shoulder, sending him flying backward. A shot rang out, echoing like thunder across the cavernous atrium.

Kara watched in horror as Lyra soared into open air—she was trying to jump from one side of the atrium to another, a space of several hundred feet! The cat wasn't even halfway across when she lost momentum. She was going to plummet three stories with nothing to break her fall but the hard floor below!

Suddenly two iridescent golden wings fanned open from the cat's back! Lyra flew across the wide-open space and crashed to the floor by Kara's feet. The magical wings shimmered, folded close, and vanished.

Sobbing uncontrollably, Kara buried her face in Lyra's thick coat.

"We have to move," Lyra urged. *"Now would be a good time."*

Kara looked up to see the astonished police running around the circle toward them. She jerked back sharply. "Oh no!" Her hands were full of blood. Lyra's blood.

Out of the corner of her eye, she saw something move. The unicorn! It was leaping from mirror to mirror, running toward an emergency exit at the end of the hall.

"I have to get you to Emily!"

Lyra stumbled to her feet and lurched forward. Kara helped the cat stay upright as they staggered down the hall. Reaching the door, Kara slammed into the security bar. The door flew open and a piercing alarm began to wail.

Kara and Lyra tumbled down two flights of steps and burst into another hallway.

"There! That side door!" Kara pointed. She urged Lyra forward, moving down the mirrored hall. Kara looked over her shoulder. No sign of any police. They were going to make it!

Thunder boomed and the lights dimmed. Kara saw herself reflected in the darkened mirror. Suddenly the reflection twisted, her face becoming strange and sneering. It was not her own image at all, but that of an older woman with silver-blond hair and the hypnotic, slitted eyes of an animal.

"I know who you are," the Dark Sorceress said, her voice smooth as velvet.

Kara was mesmerized. Every fiber of her being screamed at her to run, but she couldn't move. *I know who you are.* The message on her computer screen!

"You are right to be afraid." The animal-woman's words seemed to float through the air. "The banshees have foretold darkness will befall you."

"Call them off!" Kara cried. Her own voice sounded desperate to her ears, childish and high.

"Only magic can keep you safe," the sorceress continued. "But you need to make it truly yours."

"You mean with this?" Kara held up the jewel.

"Use it . . . and bring me what I seek."

"I won't let you take Lyra!"

"That pathetic beast is useless to me. You know what I want."

The sorceress jerked her finger upward, and the jewel around Kara's neck flew into the air. The chain tightened, biting into the back of her neck.

Smiling in triumph, the sorceress pointed.

Kara slowly turned. The unicorn stood in the mirror behind her. His eyes blazed with fury and desperation. The sorceress was hunting the unicorn all along. Yet there he was. Kara's heart felt like it would break as she realized using the jewel must have summoned him.

"You can take what you want. Or are you too afraid to use the jewel?" The sorceress twisted her hand, pulling the jewel closer, making Kara cry out in pain.

Her feet slid across the floor as she tried to pull away.

"Lyra . . ."

The cat lay sprawled on the floor, blood pooling under her belly.

"You do not need anyone."

"Who are you?" Kara gasped.

"Don't you recognize me, dear?" the sorceress spoke. So cool, so casual, the words held no threat, no pain, just truth. "I am you."

Kara's eyes widened.

"You want magic. I can give it to you." The sorceress's eyes blazed, and for the first time, Kara tasted the full power of the jewel—it was overwhelming.

The hallway tilted at a dizzying angle. Diamond fire burst up her legs, twisting like snakes around her arms, rocketing into her brain and into the very depths of her heart. Power rushed through her like a tornado threatening to take her off the face of the earth. Stars exploded behind her eyes as magic crackled like lightning across the mirrors.

She couldn't stop it, she didn't want to stop it. With this jewel, she could do anything her heart desired and it was all hers!

The Dark Sorceress laughed, her animal eyes blazing as she reached a long silver claw though the glass.

With a sudden blast of white light, Kara was back in the hallway. Breathless, she turned to face the unicorn. Pure and selfless, the creature was giving his magic to her, fighting to pull her back from the sorceress's grasp.

Kara clung to the unicorn's magic like a shield. She felt caught between forces she could barely comprehend. But she knew that if she succumbed to the Dark Sorceress, the unicorn would fall with her.

The jewel flared around her neck. "I am not you!" Kara cried at the sorceress. She threw her hands in front of her and the power blasted outward, every ounce of it directed at the wicked face in the mirror.

Magic exploded in the hallway, shattering the glass. Shock waves ricocheted like gunfire as silver shards flew everywhere. Kara scarcely noticed as she pulled Lyra to the door.

"Hang on, please!" Kara kicked open the exit door and dragged Lyra into a driveway behind the mall. Black clouds swirled above while a cold, damp wind whipped through the parking lot. Thunder ripped across the sky and rain began to fall.

Kara hunched over Lyra's fallen body. Rain splattered her face, mixing with her tears. "Help me! Someone help me!"

"I am here," a voice said, clean and pure as the rain.

Kara turned. The unicorn stood on the pavement not four feet away. The creature was magnificent: tall, lean, and muscular, with a lustrous white satin hide and long silky mane and tail curling in the wind. A scalloped crystalline horn protruded from its forehead, glistening with faint rainbow colors.

"Please," Kara sobbed, trying to lift the heavy cat. "I have to help my friend."

"We must ride . . ." the musical voice echoed strong and certain inside Kara's mind.

The unicorn knelt before her. Kara stared, openmouthed, as she realized the creature had come to help her.

Gasping, she pulled and pushed and managed to hoist Lyra's limp body across the unicorn's neck. The great magical beast rose, standing tall and strong, his horn glowing like a crystal beacon pointing defiantly at the darkened sky.

Gripping a handful of silky mane, Kara leaped up on the unicorn's back. With a snort and a nod of its head, the unicorn bolted. Across the pavement of the parking lot and into fields beyond they ran. Kara could no longer make out features of the landscape that flew by in a blur. Faster and faster, they galloped across the open meadow—then, with a great leap, they vanished, burning across the sky like a blazing star.

19

KARA STOOD ON a beach, watching waves rolling lazily upon the warm sands. Thick mist obscured something hidden on the horizon. Roiling clouds sparkled like distant lightning. Under a dawning sky, the wind became whispers, as dozens of willowy wraithlike figures surrounded her. Draped in delicate, flowing robes of gossamer, they had enormous eyes, exotic in the half-light. Sparkling emerald hair cascaded over faces with beautiful pale skin, smooth and flawless, untouched by age and time.

Surely she was dreaming.

"Is she the one?"

Kara heard them talking, studying her. She sensed warmth, but something else, too. Expectation? Excitement?

"The unicorn came to her!"

The wraiths swirled around her.

"She wields the jewel!"

One of them glided close to Kara, impossibly beautiful and flowing with light. Kara's fear seemed to melt away.

"Where am I?" she asked.

"You are safe here, child."

Another wraith floated around her. "The jewel you hold is the most powerful of magic. It has been lost to us for hundreds of years."

"Many have suffered trying to retrieve this jewel."

"You can't take this." Kara clutched the jewel. "I need it."

"Do you think you are ready to wield its magic?"

Kara flashed on Lyra's bleeding body somewhere at the edge of her mind. "My friend is hurt, dying because of me." She felt her cheeks wet with tears.

The wraith fluttered. "Sometimes magic brings loss."

The first wraith faced Kara. "Close your eyes, child."

Kara closed her eyes. A soft breeze dried her tears.

"Now open them."

Kara blinked and looked out at the gleaming ocean. The strange glowing mist still hid whatever lay underneath.

"Do you see any difference?"

"No," Kara said, confused.

The wraith sighed, a sound like the wind crying.

"Only those who truly understand the magic can find Avalon."

"Where is Avalon? How do we get there?"

"There are fairy maps to guide the blazing star."

Kara's heart sank. Phel had tried to give her a fairy map, and she had destroyed it. "I ruined everything, didn't I?"

"Everything changes," the first wraith said. "Changing all the time. It is the way of magic. There is always another chance to make a difference."

"I have to help my friend," Kara pleaded. "Please, let me keep the jewel."

"Go now. And when you are ready, you will find your way back to us."

"Kara!" As they sang out her name, chills coursed through her body.

"Kara . . ."

The figures swirled around her, blazing into bright ribbons of light.

"Kara, are you all right?"

Grass tickled her nose as she opened her eyes. She was lying in an open field at Ravenswood. The dark sky was filled with menacing clouds. Slowly, shapes came into focus. Ozzie was looking down at her, concerned and frightened. Adriane was touching her shoulder, her face grim.

"What happened?" Kara asked, struggling to sit up. She grasped the jewel still hanging around her neck and let out a sigh of relief.

"Storm brought us here," Adriane told her.

Kara's breath caught in her throat. "Lyra!"

"Emily's trying to heal her," Ozzie said worriedly. "But we need your help."

Across the field, Emily leaned over the still body of the cat. Ronif, Rasha, Balthazar, and some of the other animals stood nearby. Kara got to her feet and rushed to Emily's side. "Can you heal her?"

Lyra lay in the grass, her beautiful fur caked with blood.

"She's not responding to my magic." Emily wiped at her eyes, red from tears. "I couldn't help her when she was burned, either."

"Yes you did, Emily!" Kara gripped Emily's shoulders, making the girl look at her. "You healed Ozzie, you healed Ariel, you even healed Phel! You kept Lyra from dying. You can do it again."

"But I had Phel's magic to help me," Emily cried.

"And now you've got ours!" Kara held up her jewel, radiant in her hand. She called to the animals, "We need your help."

"Hurry everyone, gather 'round!" Ozzie ran about, herding the animals closer.

"Tell us what to do, Emily," Adriane pleaded.

"Concentrate as hard as you can on giving her strength."

The cat's sides barely rose and fell with her shallow breaths.

Kara tried to visualize pushing her own energy into Lyra, reviving her, healing her. Light from her jewel began to pulse between her fingers.

Ronif suddenly looked past the huddled group. "We have company."

A dozen banshees surrounded them. Rain pasted their filthy rags to their sickly glowing bodies.

"Keep focused on Lyra!" Kara ordered.

With piercing wails, the banshees began to close in on them, arms outstretched, grasping. The weeping cries broke the animals' concentration, and Lyra's breathing grew ragged and weaker.

"What do we do?" Rasha asked.

"There's too many of them!" Ozzie looked around frantically.

"You have to keep them away!' Emily exclaimed. "We need time!"

Adriane sprang to her feet. "We'll hold them back. Storm!"

"I am here." The mistwolf materialized from the shadows, golden eyes shining.

The banshees shambled forward, weeping madly. Facing the creatures, Adriane and Storm stood side by side. Arms crossed in front of her, the warrior assumed a fighting stance. Storm's eyes blazed, matching the gold light that flashed from Adriane's gem.

"Stay with me, Storm." Adriane swung her arm, streaming arcs of bright magic. She whirled around, spinning the light into a ring. Storm crouched low, teeth bared, as Adriane turned faster, building ring upon ring of magic. Faster and faster she spun, surrounded by expanding loops of golden fire.

Kara bent over Lyra and grasped Emily's hand. White diamond sparkles burst from Kara's jewel, running up and down her arms like electricity. With a wave, the magic leaped into Emily's jewel.

"Focus on her heartbeat. Keep it strong," Emily instructed. Green-blue light from her rainbow gem began to pulse in a steady rhythm.

Kara's jewel fell into sync with Emily's, flashing with the beat of their hearts.

"That's it," Emily said.

Magic streamed out of Emily's jewel, enveloping the cat in a cocoon of glowing rainbow light.

Suddenly the light shifted as if it were being pulled away. "I can't hold it!" Emily cried. The magic flew apart, spreading wildly out across the field.

Kara felt Lyra's pulse drop. "Don't let her go, Emily!"

"Hurry," Ozzie urged, watching the banshees approach.

Kara saw Adriane spinning like a top. Black hair whirling around her, Adriane began to rise into the air. She flipped into a somersault and sent the glowing rings of magic flying outward. Waves of light crashed into the banshees, knocking them back with the force of the blow. The warrior whipped golden fire into a huge ring about her head. Then with a snap of her wrist, the ring soared over the banshees and floated down around them. The warrior pulled tight, trying to keep the banshees away from Kara. Suddenly the golden magic burst apart, splintering across the open field.

The banshees scrambled forward again, reaching madly for Kara.

Power exploded from Kara's jewel, blasting diamond fire around the field. Magic zigzagged like wild lightning. Suddenly, ground trembled; the air twisted and ripped open. Amazed, the girls and animals looked into the looming maw of the portal.

20

"*T*HE PORTAL'S OPENED!" Ozzie screamed.

Glistening strands sparkled behind the thick, swirling mist that covered the portal. Wind whipped at the girls as they backed away.

The banshees staggered backward, covering their faces.

In a shimmering green flash, a black-cloaked figure took form and stepped out of the portal. Long, slender fingers drew back the hood, revealing green animal eyes and cool, porcelain skin framed by silvery hair slashed by a bolt of lighting.

It was her—the woman in the mirror. The Dark Sorceress.

"So, it has come to pass," the sorceress sneered. "Three new mages. Clumsy and inept, yet you wield magic."

Kara's blood turned to ice. She saw the animals shrinking away from the evil apparition.

The figure looked past Kara and regarded the banshees, who cowered on the ground in fear. "Persistent, I'll give you that much," she told them. She turned cold animal eyes to Kara. Her voice was soft as silk and sharp as a razor. "They've been after the jewel for some time. How interesting that you should find it, don't you think?"

"Plesszze," a hideous voice crackled. It was a banshee. It looked at Kara. "Help uszz."

"Why don't you just take it, if that's what you want?" Kara asked the sorceress.

"I can't use it," the sorceress said softly, hypnotic eyes locked on Kara's. "It was meant for you."

Kara hesitated. *Was* the jewel meant for her? It had to be! After everything that had happened, she still held it in her hand. And the power, the magic—it felt glorious!

"You know your magic is the strongest, your jewel the most powerful. Don't deny what is yours. Use the magic and fulfill your destiny."

"Kara, don't listen to her," Ozzie implored. "You heard the Fairimentals. The jewel is a trap!"

The sorceress eyed the ferret and laughed. "What a cruel joke the Fairimentals have played on you. An elf in the shape of a . . . puny rat. Do you even remember who you are anymore?"

Ozzie backed away uncertainly.

"Don't use the jewel!" Adriane called out.

"I know what you want," the sorceress urged softly. "With this magic, no one can stop you. No one can tell you what to do. Use the jewel and make it yours forever."

Kara felt the words echo in her mind, taking hold.

"Kara, no!" Emily cried.

Adriane whipped her wrist and sent a bolt of magic arcing through the air. The Dark Sorceress raised her hand and the magic splintered into sparks, raining back over the girls and animals.

With a savage snarl, Stormbringer attacked. But the great wolf passed through the cloaked body as if the sorceress were a ghost. Storm danced away, snapping.

The sorceress stared at Adriane, eyes flashing with rage. "You bond with a mistwolf!" Her blood-red lips twisted with scorn. "Bonds can be broken." She turned back to the terrified banshees. "Useless creatures." She looked at Kara. "Now you may destroy them."

Kara steeled herself. This was why she wanted to have magic. Now she wouldn't have to worry about the banshees anymore. She could stop *anyone* who got in her way.

Kara raised the jewel, then stopped. "What do you want from me?"

"You must fulfill your destiny, as the banshees foretold."

A destiny of *dark* magic, Kara realized.

"You want me to use my jewel to call the unicorn," Kara said. "You want his magic."

The sorceress smiled, revealing sharp fangs. "You know how it feels to want magic, don't you?"

Kara faltered. The Dark Sorceress was right. Magic was everything she wanted.

"Prove yourself." The sorceress's eyes blazed with an inhuman glow as she pulled the final strings of the trap. "Call the unicorn," she instructed calmly. "He cannot resist your magic."

My magic. Kara tightened her grip on the jewel. What should she do?

A banshee reached forward, clawed hand outstretched, sadness burned forever in crying eyes. "You must not take his magic."

Kara studied the ghastly face. But hideous as it was, the creature wept as if its heart was truly broken.

Some things are yours only for a short time.

Kara looked from the banshees to her friends, then at the beautiful glowing gem. "What if I never find another magic jewel? I want this to be mine!"

"Then you are truly like her!" wailed the banshee. "As it has been foretold."

To your own heart be true.

There is always another chance to make a difference.

The sorceress smiled so cruelly it made Kara sick. This was not how magic was supposed to work. How could she keep the jewel when each time she used it, it would bring her closer to being something so evil? How could she face herself? How could she face her friends?

The truth burned through Kara as powerful as any

magical force: even if she *never* found another one, this stone was not hers to keep. She was not the blazing star.

Kara lowered her hand. "You really think I'm like you?"

She felt for the clasp on her locket. The crystal hung quiet, cool, as she removed the stone—and gave it to the nearest banshee.

"No!" The sorceress's face contorted with fury. "You stupid child!"

Backing away, the banshee hissed and wrapped her clawed hands around the glowing jewel.

Kara whirled on the sorceress. "You don't know who I am."

Brilliant light streamed up into the sky, raining down over the banshees. Kara watched in amazement as the creatures began to change, their horrible faces and dirty rags transforming. The vile green glow dissolved and flowed away, revealing beautiful wraith-maidens who shone with clean, pure magic. The same wraiths Kara had just seen in her vision.

The image of the Dark Sorceress shuddered and warped, becoming transparent.

"Your magic is nothing without me to guide you," the sorceress hissed as she continued to fade. "Your precious animals will never be safe, here or on Aldenmor."

The spectral image twisted into mist and vanished.

The wraiths swirled around the girls with a sound like bells.

"We are free."

"Free of the evil spell."

"How do we stop that thing from coming back?" Adriane asked.

"You must construct a web of protection before the portal closes."

"How?" Emily asked.

Pop! pop! pop! pop! pop!

Dozens of rainbow bubbles appeared, dragonflies popping out all over, each one trailing streams of something behind them.

"What are they holding?" Emily asked.

"My hair!" Kara exclaimed.

The dragonflies zipped into the field, long strands of Kara's rainbow hair held in their mouths and paws. Fiona and Blaze darted past Kara with a dip and a wave, and Barney flapped by, glimmering lilac. The dragonflies lit the air with their shimmering eyes and an occasional tiny burst of fire. A little gold one buzzed in front of Kara's face, trailing a long strand of rainbow hair. "Keekee!"

"Goldie!" she exclaimed. "Can you build a web?"

Goldie chattered with perfect assurance and then flittered straight up above Kara's head, coughing out a fiery rallying cry. The busy little fliers tugged trailing streamers behind them like wisps of starlight, gossamer thin and glittering with raindrops. They flew off in different directions, warbling dragonfly calls and pulling the strands. Soon they had woven strands into a rainbow web.

"It's working!" Kara shouted.

"Use your jewels to power the web," the wraith said.

All around the girls, the animals gathered: quiffles, pegasi, brimbees, and jeeran. Emily and Adriane held up their jewels. The dragonflies fluttered in the air, holding the web in place over the portal.

Kara stood between her friends, arms outstretched. She reached out and touched Emily and Adriane's hands. Even without a jewel of her own, sparkling diamond light raced through her body and into the other girls' stones. This time, the magic felt right, made by a true heart and true friends.

As power poured into the strands, the dragonflies glowed more brightly, their jeweled eyes glistening like sequins. The rainbow colors of the web shimmered, and the droplets of water caught in its net sparkled like diamonds, reflecting the stars that twinkled behind in the darkness of the portal. The net stretched outward, then snapped tightly into place, perfectly woven with one hole in the center.

"Look at that!" Ozzie exclaimed.

"It looks like a—" Adriane started.

"—dreamcatcher," Emily finished.

The dragonflies had woven the strands of Kara's rainbow hair into a dreamcatcher.

"Only those who use good magic may pass through," the wraith said.

The wraiths swirled into the portal, their delicate bodies shining. As their pure magic touched the dreamcatcher, its rainbow strands flashed, strengthening the protection spell.

The portal swirled and vanished, leaving a blanket of light rain falling upon the forest. The wraiths were gone and the field was quiet.

Kara started to walk to her friends. Everyone stared, awestruck, at something behind her.

"What?" she asked in alarm.

The unicorn stood in the field, white as the purest snow. He bowed his head, horn sparkling with colors.

Kara approached the beautiful creature. "She wanted you all along, didn't she?"

"Yes."

Yet despite the risk, he had come to her. She hugged his neck, crying softly into his lustrous, smooth hide.

"I wanted your magic, too," she said, feeling an emptiness in her heart so vast, she felt she might cry forever.

"You have saved the fairy wraiths and helped all these animals."

"Now I have nothing," Kara sniffled.

"It is time for the magic to be renewed," the unicorn said. "You are the blazing star."

Kara's eyes widened. With a touch as soft as a kiss, the pain was gone. She lifted her head. "Will I see you again?"

"Yes. Go to your friends. They need you now."

Diamond light flared from the unicorn's horn. The magical creature reared back on his hind legs, magnificent and free. In a flash of light, he vanished.

Kara turned back to Emily, Adriane, and the animals. In the center of the group sat Lyra, green eyes flashing.

"Are you all right?" Kara ran over to the big cat.

"*Seems so.*" Lyra rubbed her head against Kara's cheek.

Emily smiled. "She's a little weak, but she'll be just fine."

"I was so scared." Kara hugged Lyra tight. "I thought I'd lost you."

"*You saved the unicorn,*" Lyra said. "*The most powerful of all magical creatures.*"

"Yeah, and I lost all my magic."

"*Not quite.*" The big cat gazed at Kara, waiting.

"Hey! I can still talk to you!" Kara exclaimed. "Even without the jewel!"

The cat looked at her, warmth and love in her eyes. "*Is that okay?*"

"Yes, it's okay!" Kara turned to her friends and shouted with joy. "I can still talk to her!"

Emily, Adriane, and the animals all smiled back.

"You did an amazing thing, Kara, giving your jewel to those fairy creatures," Ozzie said.

But Kara knew how close she had come to taking the unicorn's magic. The temptation to keep the jewel had nearly blinded her, but she had made her choice. She would choose to work with her friends and protect all magical creatures. Even without the jewel, she was the blazing star. Whatever magic she had was inside her, something no one could take away.

21

*K*ARA SAT BACK in the soft leather chair, her laptop open beside her, feet propped up on an ornate
footstool that stood on carved animal paws. She was in a
pleasant sun-drenched sitting room overlooking the
great lawn of Ravenswood Manor.

Kara shook out her restored blond hair. She was feeling better. For the first time in days, nobody was trying
to kill her. She had been frantic about not showing up at
home Saturday after that incident at the mall. But no one
noticed. Her parents had been at the country club all day.
Kara was in the clear. No one yelled, and she wasn't
grounded. Another amazing magical moment. The only
one upset was Kyle when he found out he'd missed all the
action at the mall.

goodgollymolly: u ditched us at the mall
kstar: sry about that, I had to make sure the cat got
back to ravenswood safely
credhead: the whole mall shut down lol

Kara winced. The cat showing up at school was one thing, having it run around the mall being chased by police was totally different. Even if the gunshot was accidental, the town council was not going to be happy, especially Mrs. Windor, who would use this as more ammunition to try to close down the preserve. The website just *had* to work!

Emily and Adriane had spent the last two days detailing the site. Now that they had the old Ravenswood files as their base, the work went much faster. The data for the public access section of the site was finished and ready. They had an explanation of the RWPS, its mission to protect and educate about wildlife and endangered species, plus directions to Stonehill and Ravenswood. Emily was working on adding a section of pet tips and a list of animals on the tour.

Then there was the second, password-encoded level. They had begun to add a compilation of everything they had learned so far about magic. Combining that with files already on the system, it was quite a collection, from sketches of the duck-like quiffles that Adriane had drawn, to a catalog of magic jewels and animals, and pictures of beautiful dreamcatchers, like the one that now protected the portal.

> **goodgollymolly:** u don't care about us anymore :(
> **beachbunny:** what do you see in them?
> **credhead:** it's not like they give good parties and they're pretty far down the food chain as far as clothes go
> **kstar:** so they don't know clothes, that's not everything

There was silence. All IMs ceased ringing. Maybe she had gone too far with that one. But she was sure now of one thing.

> **kstar:** Ravenswood is really important to me. U know, credhead's got singing lessons, ggmolly's helping her mom with catering, bbunny has dance class, pretty soon we'll be trying out for all sorts of stuff. Does that mean we stop being friends?
> **goodgollymolly:** no :)

"Kara, we're almost ready!" Adriane shouted down the hall.

Kara closed down her IMs with an unaccustomed feeling. Was there anyone who really understood her?

The door pushed open and Lyra walked into the sitting room. Her spotted fur shone in the sunlight streaming through the big windows.

"Where have you been?" Kara asked, annoyed.

Lyra stretched hugely. *"I thought you would like some space."*

"I don't need space." Kara glanced at the cat and back to the screen. "I like company."

"Really? I hadn't noticed." The big cat padded over and plumped down next to Kara's chair.

Kara sighed and gently scratched Lyra's neck. "It's just I always have all this stuff going on, school, friends, parties, and shopping. Before, I didn't have to choose, I was like a passenger in a car." She looked at the cat. "But now, this time . . . I'm driving the car." She pouted. "I don't know how to drive. I'm too young."

"Maybe you are too young," Lyra agreed. The big cat gazed evenly at the blond-haired girl. *"But you made a good choice, and I have faith that you will make more good choices."*

Kara smiled and gestured to her backpack sitting on the floor. "You like cat food?"

Lyra sniffed. *"Then again I could be wrong."*

"Kara, come on!" Adriane called out.

"Okay!" Kara called back. She shut down her laptop, picked up her backpack, and ran down the hall.

In the library, Adriane and Emily sat at the console looking at the RWPS homepage. Storm was stretched out by the window soaking up the sun. Ozzie, Balthazar, Ronif, and Rasha were examining the screen, comparing it to a printout propped up beside them.

"So, we're, like, live?" Kara asked, laying her backpack on the table.

Emily smiled. "As soon as we connect to the council's server."

"That's great. What about the second level?"

"All we have to do is enter our password, and we'll have access," Adriane said.

"Anyone else who knows the password will be able to access us, too," Emily added.

They all looked at the keypad.

"Okay, are we ready?" Emily asked excitedly.

"Not quite," Kara said, standing beside the table.

Emily and Adriane looked at her.

"Before we open the site to the world . . ." The girls and animals studied her curiously. " . . . While this is still ours, at least for the next few minutes . . . I just wanted to . . . I mean, I thought we could—oh, never mind." Kara opened her backpack, pulled out a small box tied with a pink ribbon, and handed it to Emily. "This is for you."

Emily's eyes went wide. Adriane gave the gift a quick glance.

"Is it my birthday already?" Emily giggled.

"Go on, just open it," Kara instructed.

Emily untied the pretty ribbon, opened the box, and lifted out a sparkling silver bracelet. "Kara . . . it's beautiful!"

"Yeah, the clasp will hold your jewel securely around your wrist, see?" Kara helped Emily remove the jewel from its woven setting, attach it to the silver clasp, and lock the bracelet.

Emily held her arm up. The bracelet and jewel were a dazzling combination. "I love it, Kara. Thank you," she said, beaming.

Kara smiled, then looked at Adriane who quickly turned away as Kara reached in her backpack and held out another box.

"I can't take your gift," Adriane said, eyes downcast.

"Yes, you can, and you will!" Kara ordered. "If you're going to keep doing all that fancy jumping and flying stuff, how do you expect your jewel to stay in place, huh?"

Adriane's mouth twitched in a smile.

"Take it . . . please." Kara held out the box. "I want you to have it."

Adriane slowly took the box from Kara. She opened it and held up an exquisite black wristband inlaid with turquoise.

"This is too much . . ." Adriane gasped.

"You like it?"

"I . . . yeah, I do."

"You're welcome." Kara smiled at her.

Adriane smiled back.

"How could one ferret be so right?" Ozzie burst out. "I think I might cry!"

All three girls looked at the ferret.

"I've found all three mages, the healer, the warrior, and the blazing star! How great am I?"

They all laughed, bound together by the magic they shared and the friendship they were learning to trust.

"Okay! Let's get this club happening!" Kara exclaimed.

Emily sat at the console and connected to the council server.

Adriane stood next to Kara. "Remember when I told you the magic didn't like you?"

"Vaguely."

"I was wrong," Adriane admitted.

Kara arched an eyebrow. "Even though I gave it back?"

"It likes you *because* you gave it back," Adriane said.

Kara and Adriane smiled at each other. Emily couldn't help but smile, too, as the connection was made.

"Congratulations, ladies and gents!" Emily announced. "The RWPS homepage is live. I think it would only be fitting that our esteemed president be the one to officially open the magic web." She grinned at Kara. "Would you do the honors, please?"

Kara smiled at her friends and typed in the password that would announce to the world they had arrived: Avalon.

WELCOME TO
RAVENSWOOD WILDLIFE PRESERVE
Open 11 A.M. to dusk

Please stay on the paths and don't feed the animals.
Take only pictures and leave only footprints.

Here, we are all explorers and students of nature.
We all have a role in protecting our natural world
and every creature that lives there. If we care for
the earth, these special friends and wild places
will be preserved and available for our families
and future generations to enjoy.

THE RAVENSWOOD WILDLIFE
PRESERVATION SOCIETY CREED:

- Respect our planet and all life forms we share
  with it.
- Preserve endangered and threatened animals
  and their habitats.
- Protect wild animals and wild places.
- Save all wonders of the living natural world.
- Value the wilderness and the wild things that
  live there.

BESTIARY
& CREATURE GUIDE

Lyra, Magic Cat

AFFILIATION: Good

Lyra is an exotic leopard-like magical winged cat. Only those with magic can see her magnificent wings. The magic cats of Aldenmor vary in size and coloring and possess a keen intelligence, sharp intuitive senses, and deep empathy for others.

Unicorn

AFFILIATION: GOOD

*U*nicorns are the most legendary and powerful of all magical animals—highly sought after and coveted by those seeking magic. Fast as lightning, unicorns can run upon the magic web itself, transporting themselves and their rider anywhere on the web without the need of a portal.

DRAGONFLY

AFFILIATION: NEUTRAL

*D*ragonflies are miniature dragons originally bred in the Fairy Realms. Their magic derives from fairy magic, giving them unique abilities. They can pop anywhere without the need of a portal and can communicate between worlds. Being fairy in nature, dragonflies are fun-loving and playful. Wild dragonflies basically spread magic seeds and rarely ever bond with humans.

Water Fairimental

AFFILIATION: Good

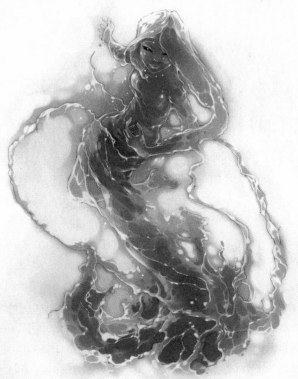

*F*airimentals are elemental beings, protectors of the good magic of Aldenmor. They take form and shape from one of four elements: air, water, earth, and fire. Fairimental magic is tied to Aldenmor, and they can appear only for very short amounts of time on Earth.

Rachel Roberts on Writing, Best Friends, and Elephants

"**A**VALON—WEB OF MAGIC" is Rachel Roberts' first series of novels. She says most ideas for her stories and characters come on long hikes with her best friend, Ensign, a silver white husky. She carries a small notepad for jotting down thoughts and discussing with Ensign. Then at home she expands on the ideas with cat pals, Attila and Raider.

Rachel is an avid campaigner for animal rights. "My secret wish: I'd love to adopt an elephant, but I know wild animals need to be in their natural environment or in the proper care of professionals for the animal's own best interests—and probably my neighbors'. Oh well, elephants are still cool."

Westminster Public Library
3705 W. 112th Ave.
Westminster, CO 80031
www.westminsterlibrary.org